"Wow, my entire life was a waste."

Dead, his soul floating in the limitless void, and very bored, our hero's prior life seemed tasteless.

Life was about to turn around for our hero. He had published two light novels before, "Help! The Girls School has Made Me Their Dog" and "My Antisocial Sister is a Succubus", and his next one received a lot of support and enthusiasm, in the form of his publisher breathing down his neck. His mother was willing to pay for the first few months of rent after he left the basement. He was even on the way towards the path to having a girlfriend.

If only that truck hadn't hit him.

"Thank God it's over. My life was a waste. I'm short and fat. I couldn't make money as a light novelist. My dad thought I was gay. Not an hour before I came to a cosplayer's thighs.

"Every time I said I would do better, I gave up and stuck to my old habits. When I knew what was the right thing to do, I ignored my better self. Now I'm dead, and I didn't experience what most people get to experience: happiness, friendship, love. Or, at least, what most of my characters get to experience.

"If I get a second life, I'd change things around. I mean, I died, so I know there's nothing worse than that." So he thought, bored in the void.

He was then dragged down, as if an invisible whirlpool were drawn beneath his feet. He tried paddling with his arms in the wind and calling for help. He was taken through a corridor of stars, and finally emerged into a brilliant white light.

Where the void had been only black, this world was a luminous white, almost painfully bright. Sitting on a stool, a beautiful woman with a lofty addressed him.

"Greetings. As you should know, you are dead. Normally you would travel to an appropriate afterlife, but I have been tasked to make offers to similar souls as you: an offer to live in another world ..."

She had amazing breasts. They were magnificent breasts in the world prior, and any world he would experience after. Her breasts were so sufficient no other were needed. They were fantastic regardless of the angle or the pose one caught her in; in fact, they were so big they could not be obscured, regardless of where one was in the room. They were sufficient in bankrupting every milkman. In a sense they were like two gods, of beauty, of bounciness. They were like bunnies trying to escape from her flimsy dress, they were like fruit heavy on a bough, they were majestic waterfalls of flesh. He was genuinely afraid they would fall sheer off her body, leaving her breastless, but no less beautiful. He wanted every part of his body to touch those breasts.

"... and upon defeating the demon lords you will be richly rewarded. What do you say?"

"Yes."

"On returning back to life?"

"Absolutely, yes."

They smiled and shook hands.

"You have the softest hand I have ever touched," he said.

She smiled and gazed at him inquiringly.

2

Our hero was rinsed in light. He felt his body soar through space, through time, through consequence, to a destination he knew not, because he had not been listening.

He thought only of his new life. What he most wanted to be was an adventurer, the kind he often read about in books and saw in movies. These were strapping young men, strong, well-traveled, who searched the ends of the earth for knowledge and treasure, and often met bosomy women in very thin clothing, some pure, some dangerous, but all finding the hero irresistible. This kind of life was so good he was surprised it was virtually nonexistent in the prior world.

Or, as often happens in this genre, he would be reborn as some kind of fantastical being, perhaps a monster, a goblin, a living slime, or a spider. Oppressed all of his life by those who regarded himself as the superiors of him and his fellow beings, he would break the shackles of persecution, repulse his oppressors, prove his worth to a hateful world, thereby freeing the world of hate, and in the aftermath and most likely throughout his adventures make love to many lovely, swoonable ladies, who were hopefully human and willing.

"This will be a good life. Because I have never had wealth, I'll try my hand at being wealthy; because I have never known love, I'm going to be loved; because I have never put myself out, I'm going to be surrounded by friends; because I have never read a book, in this world I'm going to know many things. The world is going to be happy because I'm going to have a happy outlook."

It was thus a great misfortune that he was born as himself. He expected and desired so greatly a different type of life than his worst one that he considered dying again.

The world around him was lush with life. Around the plain he had been reborn in, deer capered, boar scoured for mushrooms, and insects danced happily in the air, for it was the season of growth. He felt the sensual warmth of sunshine on his belly and the soft stalks of grass flat on his feet. The air was sweet compared to the thick smoke of the city. At the end of the horizon was endless blue sky, untainted by human hands. For a moment, he paused from his despair of being born himself again and took in the joys of nature.

Nature decided then to rain. He felt the sudden downpour on his head, his stomach and his thighs. He now understood he was naked. He retreated to the shelter of a tree. This tree inhabited an insect. This insect was of a species possessing six hundred wings, a thousand eyes, and ten thousand mouths, and it possessed the same height as our hero, was maybe a bit taller. Fortunately this individual was a bitsmaller than the other members of his species, so it was a few inches less terrifying.

The insect startled our hero, and our hero startled the insect. The insect leapt into the mouth of a basilisk (a serpent with the head of a rooster, purportedly able to kill with a glare), which flew into the jaws of a manticore (a creature with the head of a man, the body of a lion, and the tail of a scorpion), which ran into the throat of a Mongolian death worm (an immense worm said to kill from a distance with venom), which slithered into the talons of a roc (a bird immense enough to hunt elephants), which escaped lest it found itself in the clutches of a bogwent (I do not know what this is). Higher it flew, gathering up immense gusts of wind, spraying water over our hero. Our hero sneezed, and felt he would die. He made up his mind then and there to make enough money to have clothing and shelter in this new world so as to stay far, far away from nature.

A band of pigs passed our hero by. The sow was wise during these storms and held an immense leaf in her snout to shield her brood from the wet. Our hero, having witnessed a lesson in the survival of the fittest, was given a choice, which he chose. He crawled on all fours and pretended he was one of the pigs, as many in his prior life called him, for he was not fit, and yet he wanted to survive.

These same pigs were caught in a trap. In the distance, shrouded by the rain, he saw three dark hunters approach them, twice as tall as our hero, and broad with muscles. Our hero gave a sigh of relief, for these three men would save him. They would free him, teach him their feral ways, he would develop abs, and he would be on his way to becoming an adventurer. He knew the god of this world was kinder than the one in the last.

The three sisters did take him to their home with the other pigs. They took a glance at our hero's body, and was pleased by it, as a white virgin gilt was rare, and would make for an excellent sacrifice on the next new moon.

Our hero was fond of the sisters for two reasons.

The first reason was that they fed him. Twice a day, the sisters threw ears of corn and soy bean pods into the pig pen. The pigs would saunter from their poorly-built shed, which barely kept away the elements, and devoured the sisters' produce. Our hero followed them, as he had been using their bodies for warmth, to find that most of the food was eaten by the time of his arrival; he had only the corn husks and the shells to eat. The pigs would then file back to the shed and sleep the day away, or fight in the pen, which our hero avoided by covering his head and raising his hindquarters, which gesture appeased them.

The second reason was that they were beautiful. Our hero did not see much Amazonian in them, and likened them more to Woman's Basketball. He longed to one day be free, become the adventurer he longed to be, with the abs he longed to have, and win one or all of their hearts over, in spite of their height, their elongated canines, and their hairy armpits, and have one or all sit on his face.

The sisters kept our hero in the pen by tying a silk cord around his neck, so he could not stray far. Our hero thought this was for the best. Though he did not like the other pigs, did not like their snoring, did not like the bruises they inflicted on him, did not like wading through their feces, he knew that fate decided to keep him close to the sisters as otherwise he would have run away from these primitive females.

This was not untrue. Had our hero met their brothers, he

would been ravished, disemboweled, and eaten, not
necessarily in the same order, some steps more than once,
and the sisters had many brothers, cousins, aunts, uncles
that prowled the forest in various states of mind, of various
degrees of humanity, and were colored with various shades of
brutality.

The eldest sister woke up one day with a good plan, so
good she began conversation with it. Our hero, compared to
the other pigs, was scrawny and small. She was also sick,
and her diarrheal stools made the other pigs sick as well.
They intended to sacrifice her as soon as possible, but the
rain had not let up for days, sacrifices could not be made on
rainy days, and the new moon had passed. Worst of all, she
had a protuberance over her genitals that disallowed her from
mating. She would cut this protuberance, allowing our hero to
mate; and if she died, there would be no loss.

Without a word in reply, not willing to wait any longer, she
took a cleaver, our hero, and a male pig to a back room
bloody from the slaughter of other pigs. She raised the dulled,
blood-crusted cleaver up, with an eye toward our hero's
genitals, which effect, oddly, aroused him. Just as she were to
bring it down, she recalled today was the first song of the
season, and left with little sense of caution in her mind.

Our hero believed fate saved him once more and he could
now escape with his manhood intact. Unfortunately the other
pig in the room had long been drawn to our hero, his
demureness and his slenderness, and seized the opportunity
presented to him. He pinned our hero down with his legs. Our
hero felt something long, thin and worm-like poke his behind.
He imagined a train passing through a tunnel, a thermometer
placed into a turkey, a Q-tip thrust into an ear, and a hot dog

slid into a bun.

The boar thrust. The worm bounced off. The boar thrust again. The worm bounced off again. To the boar's horror and our hero's delight, his bottom was too narrow to fit in the boar's worm. Frustrated, the boar set his mind to what he intended to do, regardless of his being unable to accomplish it; a liquid then covered our hero's back and stomach, and the worm detumesced.

Our hero ran. The boar returned to his friends to complain about his awful date.

He ran and ran, through a landscape that, happily, ceased its rain. He ran to the horizon that once painted a blue sky, now mellow with a sea of clouds, through meadows and fields, through glen and grove, until he was fortunate to see, as he hoped there to be, as he saw in movies, the walls of a great city in the distance.

He was so happy he became hot with excitement, then he laid down for he was hot with fever. He rested by a tree, where he felt he might die.

4

Minutes felt like hours and hours felt like days, in the swirling ramble in his head as he lay dying. He turned white, he vomited corn husks, and he could no longer defecate.

To his fortune a wagon of doctors alighted upon him, and they were all decent gentlemen who didn't believe each and every one of their services had to be recompensated with gold. Feeling they could not move the patient for fear of risking his life, they operated on the tree trunks.

"Fie," you, dear reader, might say, a medical professional yourself, "there is no condition under which a patient could not be moved, and 'twere there one, it is not this." I, who am merely the storyteller, and learned no skill in storytelling college except for the art of telling stories, say, Good on you, and good if you told these doctors too, because there was a dire need among them for knowing, none in more dire need than their patients.

"All disease is bloodborne, thus the patient needs less blood." He then cut several veins, spilling as much blood as possible, such that the ground was crimson red, then a rust brown. Unfortunately, this method helped him little.

"Because the body and the mind are interconnected, the patient can be cured by relieving mental duress." He drilled a hole into our hero's head, piercing the skin and stopping right at the plate of the skull. Unfortunately, this method did not help our hero's stress, and thus helped him little.

"Most diseases arise from the bowels and kidneys." He had

our hero ingest a laxative. This helped our hero little, though it gave him great gas.

"The planets are out of alignment, thus causing illness." He then folded his arms and did nothing, as he was unable to move stars. This helped our hero little.

"The testicles are the source of male vitality, ergo overstimulating the body with activity." He raised a knife, yet was distracted by an argument between two doctors. One doctor argued that those who believed disease originated from the stars were ignoramuses. It was clear that disease was contingent on the cards he drew.

The doctors perceived that our hero was dying. Some posited that death, in fact, was a cure. Some posited there was no such thing as death. Some posited that they tried their best. All, however, wanted credit for their own cure, and so they took our hero to a healer, who is a kind of spellcaster.

Spellcasters are few and far between in these lands. The city had no college of mages, as the citizens found them a suspicious bunch. However, the city had one; in fact, he was well-renowned in this land and others.

The healer dismissed the doctors, who were shouting the methods of their cures, which did somewhere between sixty to eighty percent of the work of healing our hero, which claims they advertised outside of their clinics. The healer, as a ritual, drank half of a bottle of whiskey, cured our hero with a spell, then drank the other half of the bottle, for he greatly enjoyed whiskey.

For this is the world our hero had been reborn into, a world of magic, where those who have learned to manipulate intangible, ill-defined concepts were given awesome power, the greatest of which is to charge their customers exorbitant fees for the work of lifting but a finger, which fees create an inferior class of practitioners of alternative medicines, whose services are called upon not for their correctness but for their cheapness, all contributing to a social hierarchy that could only exist in this fantastical world and surely does not exist in any other world.

Fortunately the healer did not ask our hero for a fee, as he was too drunk to recall it.

He noticed the cuts to our hero's wrists; he covered them in bandages. He noticed the hole in our hero's head; he gave him a hat. He saw the brown stains on his buttocks; he was not a nanny.

The healer allowed our hero to sleep in the bed upstairs; he remained in the living room, opening a new bottle of whiskey, and drank it while staring at a mirror the long night through, as he was wont to do every night.

Our hero awoke to an empty house, no letter conveying how he had gotten there nor the means by which he was cured. He was glad in his heart and felt, after all his earlier pains, he was fortunate he had not died yet, as there was time yet to redeem himself in the eyes of his healer, by saving the world once, maybe twice. He entered the city and looked for himself a job.

5

Allow me the opportunity to describe the city. Some things I will say, you will dislike; though I hope not to take too long, you should know this happened a long, long time ago, and the city in the present day is much happier. This is not true, but if you felt warmth in your heart hearing it, then it is true.

In the great buildings lived the nobles. In the greatest building lived the king. A king is a man who spends many hours on his throne, saying things, and sometimes those things are believed and acted upon. When they are not, he tells his guards, who are strong and armed, to make it so, and they obey, because they are paid by him.

This is what is meant when the king asserts he is the most powerful man in the realm: he is listened to by others. For those of you readers who have wives or girlfriends, you know what it is like to *not* have power.

Nobles have some relation to the king, by inheriting a blood relation or by purchasing one. They have power in that, when they wish to do something, the king sometimes does not interrupt them. Sometimes he forgives them if their actions have dire consequences, though many a wise man and many wise books say kings should be merciless, and kings like to be wise.

In smaller buildings lived everyone else, who are given no power, except concerning their own life. This was a good social contract, as they had no need for power. They had so little need for power that they often gave it up so as to be in a deficit, because they were much happier listening to other people's demands, at least, so they were told.

Let me describe a common routine in the city. A man desires food and drink, which are alien needs to the nobles. He opens his pockets; he has none. He sees other people with food and drink, but, because they have so few of it themselves, they, reasonably, deny him. This man is simple, but he is not stupid. He recognizes that, in an ideal world, he has something to give to them, so as to compensate their own time in acquiring food. He wishes he could till and farm land; alas, he has no land; he wishes he could in some way acquire raw materials and create things people would need, as shoes and tools; alas, he has no materials; he wishes he could perform some service for people, even as humbling as cleaning their shoes; alas, he has no tools. He turns to the nobles of the city, who have much gold in their possession; he wishes to be in service to them, for some gold. His service, however, is valueless to them. His right to own property, to own his employment, and to own his wages, all of which in effect allow him to own his destiny, are slightly more valuable. He then sells these things to a noble. (In truth, he would not speak to the nobles, but rather their surrogates, as they are often too busy riding horses, attending picnics, enjoying their lives, essentially.) In return, he is given a receipt of sale; the noble has his own reproduction.

Thus, every morning, the man takes this receipt, demonstrates it to a workmaster, who then gives him a menial task, as finding a needle in a haystack, or counting the grains of sand in an hourglass, or watching paint dry, for some bread, some drink, and some lodging that night, for he had none before he approached the workmaster. When the workmaster denies him work, and therefore food, he chastens the man, saying that he gave him food yesteryear, and should be grateful he is so lucky. Astounded by the moral wisdom of the workmaster, the man turns away without any food but is grateful he is surrounded by such upstanding people.

As his stomach grumbles, and he is subjected to his human needs, and he fears his time on earth is short, he finds time to scoff at his fellow man who does not rely on receipts. In truth, all men of his birth and status have receipts, but some are lost in bureaus, thrown away, or used to wipe duck fat off of the nobles' lips. Some of these free men cursed themselves for losing their receipts, and longed to find a noble who would purchase them. Some of them, through extraordinary luck, had the means to acquire something by which they could deliver goods and services unto others. Unfortunately, they were unable to sell their wares at the quantity and the price they liked, so as not to compete with the nobles' businesses, and thus they were unlikely to be much happier than their fellows.

There must be a word for a class of citizen whose freedom has been entirely given away, such that these individuals are homeless in the outskirts of the law and justice, subjected to the cruelties of the wilderness of the human soul, that being their masters'. Alas, the word, if it exists, eludes me.

The kings and the nobles liked this system. The system had been with them since the time of their ancestors, which meant it was a good idea, and less rights meant less to think about when flogging the citizens.

Outside of the city were smaller towns and villages, who were protected in part by the city. They hoped to be so small that they were ignored by more powerful people, and often this was the case.

The folk of the forest, who were given a subtle intelligence alongside their brutality, scoffed at the humans, found them inferior, and attacked the citizens often on the basis of their contempt, which necessitated the city's tall walls, for they believed in the law of the strongest, which law the king liked so much that he made it his law too. For the king was an optimist at heart, and thought good ideas came from many sources, and the goodness of an idea was proportionate to how much it made him happy.

If you, the reader, find anything of this objectionable, then let me paint you a different picture: the people of the city are happy, and spend all of their days baking bread, watching their children play, knitting sweaters, and being good neighbors. They are happy because the wealthy among them treat them well, give them good employment, thereby sharing the fortune of their wealth in exchange for honest hard work, and do not think themselves above them. The king is a just man, who abstains from relying on his heavy hand, and indeed nothing compels him to be a king, no privilege and no pleasure, except for the joy that comes from ruling his people justly and wisely. There is no disease, for mages cured it; there is no war, for mages stopped it; and there is no hierarchy, for mages like to share. The citizens are content being human, and the forest folk are content being forest folk, and people have many good reasons to be happy, for there is no reason to be sad.

If you like this picture, know that I like this picture too. I stare at it fondly and with a wide smile on my face, when I take pauses from reading this tale to you, for the picture of the world of our hero is not like this picture at all.

Our hero was fortunate to find a recruiter. Even more fortuitous was that our taskmaster had a very long list of jobs which were in demand and no one wanted, and a free afternoon that hitherto consisted only of staring at the sole beer he could afford, and he tried to abstain from drinking until lunchtime.

Our hero was pleased with the list the recruiter produced. Finally, he would be a valued member of society, with a role others considered intelligent and good, and attractive. He thought that, if he was not destined to be an adventurer this life, then surely he was given an opportunity to correct the mistakes of his last one. He chose the most honorable profession on the list.

Our hero did not do very well as a doctor. He did not have enough strength to cut through flesh and bone, which was the primary role of doctors in the new world, and he could not bear administering mercury to children or pregnant women.

He did not do very well as an attorney. Much of an attorney's day involved visits from the king's men, who had very strong opinions concerning trials, and broke several bones if the attorneys disagreed, and other bones when they were very bored.

Neither did he do well as a tutor. It was not a difficult job, as the city folk knew so little, that they did not know they were being taught anything. However, they largely paid in pies that were spoiled. They further did not like being taught how to draw manga.

He did not do very well as an accountant. It was not a difficult job, as nobles enjoyed lying about the heights of their wealth, yet when it came to paying him, they suddenly had empty pockets.

He did not do very well as an engineer. He felt there was no safe way to make buildings and bridges out of sawdust, and felt this was related to the reason why the last engineer was executed.

He did not do very well as a computer programmer. No one understood how his job was of any use.

Our hero did not do very well as a therapist. He felt that people led worse lives than he did, and yet he felt he was living in the worst one.

He did not do very well as a census taker. Half of the citizens did not know their birthdays, half of the citizens were too inebriated to care, and half of the citizens punched his face.

He did not do very well as a recruiter. He asked the recruiter, if the labor market was able to regulate itself, why it was so difficult to find competent workers for certain jobs, and why certain professions, being unable to attract quality talent, did not improve their conditions. The recruiter wondered this all his life.

The string of bad jobs was, overall, an experience. Fortunately, the recruiter earned eighty-percent of his wages. As he went to the place for each job, he walked by the Adventurer's Guild, understanding quietly that he desired most in this new world to enter the doors of that building, pick up his sword, and fight monsters with his brave companions. He held onto this wish as he went through his day, and it was here that his madam offered him a role. The most attractive part of this opportunity was that she did not need the clothes he did not own, though he did need to take a loan out for a nipple ring.

It did not take long for a client to come in through the door and choose him. This patron had an unusual appearance: as a witch had cursed him, half of his body was of a pig's.

As a result of his brutish appearance, he abandoned any pretense of being a gentle lover. He pinned our hero to the stained, lice-infested bed and made to thrust in his genitals, which also resembled a pig's. Less than a minute of hiding the cucumber, our hero felt this job was not meant for him and ran to the madam to resign. This was not difficult to do, as it took the customer less than a minute to relieve himself.

Our hero's resignation was unfortunate for the next client, who had been negotiating with the brothel's madam during the passion play. On a business trip from the forest, the pigman had been looking for some relief.

6

To our hero's luck, as he was fleeing the brothel, he had been propositioned for a job. Coming forward from the alley, the man longed to recruit prostitutes, but none were so bold to try it. He produced a glass vial of white powder and explained that he needed this vial delivered from one end of the city to the other. However, security had tightened as of late, and a number of courtiers had already been caught. He needed this vial transported through a specific, concealed place, that was sure to pass through all checks.

When our hero heard the sum rewarded, he accepted, though reluctantly. It did not matter the vial was bigger than his last lover's member.

It did not matter in the sense that it did not dampen our hero's zeal. Our hero realized there was a limit to how much the vial could be pushed in, before it triggered flatulence, then vomiting.

When it was told the king that his subjects were taking fairy's foot, wasting the strength of their limbs and spending much of their day in a doze, rather than using those same muscles to bring in wealth for the city, he furiously took his scepter, ready to lay the law of the land. However, after a reasonable discussion with some wealthy individuals, he proposed a tax on the drug in those parts of the city where recreation was the highest. This was much less barbaric, he reasoned, than cutting off the perpetrators' heads, whipping their wives and children into ribbons, and dashing any relations of theirs and friends who have shared wine onto the rocks, though, unfortunately, it was less fun.

Our hero approached a checkpoint, guarded with armed men with blades, when they were implementing a novel idea. Upon our hero alighting them, he was ordered to strip himself naked. This idea was a good one because there were a number of beautiful women in the district.

Fear coursed our hero's veins, and he bristled, as he was able to conceal the vial but to the head. Yet, being a good citizen, he complied, sitting down to take off his shoes. This had the effect of sliding the vial all the way through. Curiously, he felt it in his stomach and in his groin. He tried not to cry, though he could have if he wanted, as he seemed the sort to cry easily.

Just as, to our hero's fortune, he passed inspection, a guard noted loudly how large his buttocks were. The minds of most men are a fog, and one could not say whether he said so out of some masculine obsession or whether, indeed, they were very large buttocks. The other men began grabbing our hero's rear, slapping it, and remarked how wide it was, the size of some of the holes in their rooms. Someone called out for a banana, and they were making bets.

As soon as the tip of the banana slid in, a loud wind, a tempest, emitted from there, and the noise and the smell reminded these men they were on duty. Luckily, the vial did not fall out, but our hero retched a few times.

Our hero arrived at a lavish mansion. There were many beautiful fruits to eat here, and many beautiful women, and our hero contained within him a thing worth more than them all together, so much so that it was difficult for him to avoid attention, as he made his way over to a pot. After he relieved

himself, vial in hand, he made his way to the owner of the
mansion, who, unfortunately, had been assassinated by his
advisor. The advisor asked one of the beautiful women to
clean up the blood, only for himself to be gutted in return; so
on and so forth, until the mansion was empty save for our
hero and one acned boy, barely thirteen years of age, who
had been accustomed to taking naps around this time of day.

7

The seeds of fairy's foot, it was said, originated from one of the older gods. During a journey that lasted an eternity and then some, the goddess shed silvery tears while mourning the death of her lover which, descending to the earth, took mortal form and grew as yellow stalks with white follicles and purple-blue flowers. Notwithstanding she accepted many more lovers after, the sap from these tokens of her fidelity, when drunk, slowly closed the mind off access to every limb, then shut off the mind itself, and rendered its victim in a state of paralysis such that they would die to the elements or a predator or to eventual deprivation. Diluted, it was a favorite drug for nobles with much time on their hands and a good sedation for uppity servants.

And so our hero and the boy entered a partnership and became quite wealthy. The acned boy woke in the afternoon, gave orders until three, ate large meals, satisfied himself with girls, partook in his own wares, stalked town, ordered the death of at least one unfortunate man, and fell back to sleep long after midnight. For this, he became very well-respected.

Our hero had a much different routine. He woke up early in the morning, as he often did when working on a light novel, exercised certain essential muscles in the lower body, and allowed himself to be yelled at several times in the day, sometimes the same hour. He never stepped foot into the mansion again, was given a flat on loan, and submitted his diet and lifestyle to the boy, who recommended much beans and lentils.

Our hero had not so much given up the desire to be an adventurer or to have a noble profession, so much as he, at the moment, desired money more.

The irony was lost on him that, in a city that sold nothing, the most desired commodity was a sedative.

Our hero endeavored to give a gift to his benefactor, who already possessed everything in the world, whose world happened to be the size of the city.

As most of the boy's day was occupied with work, or so he argued was the case, our hero set off to buy perfume or a nice work shirt to complement his schedule. He went to several shops, and came out with one very expensive hat. For this, he was arrested.

The crime was that he perused very expensive stores. These stores were usually attended by nobles, who were the only class of citizen who could afford the wares. Because our hero was not usual, he was immediately suspect. It was an offense itself for a commoner to make more money than the aristocracy. The store proprietors tried to warn him through insults, heckling and spitting, so it was very much in our hero's blame.

He was subjected to various tortures in prison, as beatings, ripping his nails out, tapping his sack, noogying, and other miseries guards enjoyed. Because no one told him what the crime was, he did not think there was anything to admit, and so endured it, as he did when his editor resorted to these tactics. When he felt the hour was late, he related to his captors he had to return home to resume his job, that of being a drug mule. They then took him to a different room, without torture implements, and sat him at table.

Across the table was a beautiful woman with an elegant air about her. She covered the details of the case and detailed certain punishments. Our hero heard very little of this, and fancied she was the sort who would tell him not to get the wrong idea and that he was stupid.

She concluded that our hero must assassinate his benefactor, the acned boy, or lose his new life. In the same cool air she gave our hero a dagger, ordered him to conceal it in the way he knew how, and cut his benefactor's throat. Our hero left the jail in tears, sad to see the boy go.

8

Our hero, under the molten orange sun, contemplated the ancient sin of murder. To have another man slain was plainly wrong. The mansion had been newly decorated, so the accidents of death, as blood and guts, would render the maids' work moot.

Our hero walked through the streets of the city, whose citizens were entering the slow crawl to death by fairy's foot. Yes, the act of killing was wrong, and anyone who did so or is complicit in the act deserved harsh judgment. Yet, as our hero's sense of morality came largely from manga, he was unable to grasp why precisely it was wrong. From a philosophical perspective, the boy's death had little meaning in the enormous sea of the universe. Unfortunately, the universe mattered very little to our hero, who simply wanted to be paid.

In fact, if he refrained from killing, he would be executed, and his own death, dissolving the drug trade, would lead to the boy's death. Thus, killing the boy would be purchasing life at a discount, halving its price. But regardless of this happy math, the crime still weighed heavy on our hero's heart, as the boy would not be very happy dying.

As our hero had been out of sight for a few hours, the boy greeted him with the most horrendous string of insults, though there was no object to his complaints, he was merely very bored. Meanwhile girls were ordered to feed the boy beer and pat his stomach.

At the end of a better half of an hour, our hero finally had chance to speak: he had a present for him. The boy asked to see it, and stood. Face to face, our hero gave him the hat. It did not fit. Thus came another, louder, longer string of insults. The boy was relieved, as he now had a genuine complaint. This was the best gift of all.

Our hero removed the dagger from his rear and thrusted it into the boy's stomach. How did he muster the courage to do so? He imagined he was cutting into a pig that was long, long dead.

The boy's stomach burst with blood. It covered the entire room, our hero, the girls, the windows. In his rage, the boy groped for a letter opener on his desk, painted it with blood, and lunged at our hero, only to enter the blade again, as our hero still held out his hand. The boy screamed in agony, again, made his hands into fists, but could not hit our hero out of weakness from a loss of blood. Taking pity on him, our hero raised the dagger again – only to hit too low, slicing the boy's manhood in half.

The boy turned, his manhood a fountain of blood, spraying the girls with this blood, then fell headfirst and died.

Though not truly. He screamed for a few minutes more until the blood covered his mouth, drowning him.

The girls resigned that day, and our hero was promptly arrested for murder. Prison was dark and mean; the fare every day was gruel soup, every other day it was gruel sandwiches. The only recreations in prison were to throw one's feces at the other, and to die from illness and disease. The city's budget did not allow for more.

He disliked prison so much that he longed to be an adventurer, and, sword in hand, cut open the bars of the prison and freeing these fellows, who, regardless of whom they have murdered or ravished, deserved a chance to amend their ways and improve upon themselves, no matter how little this improvement might be. However, the very concept of prison seemed to contradict directly the concept of man as a temple of justice and virtue. He eventually became so despondent that the prisoners reserved their feces for happier men.

He was taken before a court, with the elegant woman, acting as prosecutor, and a judge. The judge was very old and could hardly keep his eyes open. The prosecutor put sole blame on the crime on our hero, explained the wages of murder were more murder, and admitted there were no witnesses interrogated, and no legal precedent for his crime, as no one in the city killed a man, much less a boy, at the time of twilight before, and the law did not specify when murder should not be done. Seeing this, our hero should be fined a great deal of gold, to be owed the city. When the judge awoke, he agreed, banged his gavel, which was his only true duty and chief love in life, and adjourned court. Thus our hero was a free man.

Upon receiving the fresh air and bright sunlight, he saw, driven by carriage, some friends he had made in prison. His experience would have been a great deal worse without them. They exchanged words, he thanked them, they wished him fortune, and he bade them farewell, as they were led to the gallows.

9

Thus, not long into his life in the new world, our hero had acquired a great debt, which penalty was more prison and therefore more gruel sandwiches. He reasoned that, if fate longed for him to be an adventurer, it would not saddle him with debt. He thus put his heart into absolving himself of it.

Feeling the burden of the world upon his shoulders, our hero first sought recreation. He came upon a crowd of people who seemed to be enjoying themselves. They were watching and waging bets on two men who were dicing.

For men as these, who owned no land, owned precious few things, had no education, and thus very dim command of the language, had no training in any discipline except in hauling goods of other men, they knew neither sport nor art, and understood nothing of why the dice had different faces when rolled, only that they did, and as a result did not understand that they had no control over their futures, and thus came to believe they had some control of their futures by taking the money of their fellow men through the devices of mere chance, which they did not understand. Thus dicing was their sport of choice, and they took it very seriously, as was the case when one of the competitors had been cut, on the reason he was cheating.

A woman, upon seeing our hero hungry, gave him a bit of bread to eat and beer to drink, and nominated him as a challenger. He had been cheered for and given much advice on how to roll the dice.

The advice and encouragement seemed quite effective as

he won a number of games.

Our hero was then offered further advice and encouragement, that if he kept winning games, and ruining their bets, one or all five of the fingers of his good hand could be cut off.

Our hero hoped the sweat of his hands would ruin his rolls. But each throw of his was blessed by fortune, such that he had earned four-fifths of the crowd's paltry earnings, had two men killed, and attracted every man's ire.

The woman who offered him fare laughed and introduced him to the only other game they played: she flattened his good hand on the ground, brought out a knife, and stabbed at the spaces between his fingers, moving more quickly with each iteration. As seconds became minutes and her hands became hard to see, no eye in the crowd became drawn away from the spectacle. Finally, she rested the knife away from his hand – and then brought it down on his index finger. Our hero screamed, the crowd cheered, the sight of blood shed seemed to calm them from their anger. This respite was the perfect opportunity to leave with the whole pot and their wallets.

Having taken all of his earnings, the businesswoman presented his finger in a cup of ice and directed our hero to the same healer who had cured him earlier, before escaping into the night.

10

His finger reattached, our hero renewed his efforts to pay off his debt.

The idea came to him while discussing with the healer what he did for recreation. A learned man, he answered simply that he read books, and drank. Our hero read books, though only the illustrated kind. In this new world, there were neither films nor television shows to watch. On television he would watch animated series, cooking shows, and women's basketball, as he found their limbs beautiful. The healer nodded, for, as a learned man, he knew when another man had to have his ramble.

Our hero set out with a new venture in mind. He sought the cooperation of the sisters.

It did not take long to find them. The sisters felt they had very little need to go to the city, seeing that urban life was inferior to living in the wilderness, and any sacrifice that had to be made for a natural lifestyle should be made, for it was the superior way of living. However, as self-sufficient as they were, the knives, cleavers, and swords of the city were sharper and lasted longer than their own, which comparison befuddled them. In order to have superior tools, they traveled to the city, once a month, trading in fur, produce, meat, and other goods.

They were not upset upon seeing our hero, as they did not recognize him. They did think the pig speaking was charming in its own right. As they had much time on their hands in-between hunting and eating animals, they thought this "basketball" would make for a good diversion. Our hero believed as every good businessman does: that his employees would be so grateful for this opportunity, they would finally sit on his face.

The partners fashioned a basketball out of leather, carved the court out of rock and wove uniforms out of cotton. The girls took the rules well, though our hero had to reduce the rules on fouls as the sisters thought violence improved the game.

There was only one problem: there was no other "team", so to speak.

Our hero assembled a rival team out of citizens, consisting of prostitutes and housewives, who were wives without houses to mind but plenty of children, who themselves could one day become basketball players. However, the women did not earn wages, their masters earned their wages. What they received for their efforts were balms for their boredom.

As these women were half the size of the sisters, our hero fancied this a sort of exhibition match.

Our hero tried to a muster a crowd for the match. Seeing there was not much to do, there were several people able to fill every seat. However, none of them owned any gold. Our hero settled with payment in bread.

The exhibition was a success. The crowd walked away much entertained. There was enough interest to fill the calendar year with matches.

The chief problem was that every player on the opposing team resigned, or had to resign, from concussion, broken limbs, or immoderate fear of "basketball". In fact, the audience specifically clamored for the head-breaking and the leg-bending the sisters were keen on doing.

Fortunately, there were more seats to fill around the court than there were women in a team. If the women were educated, they would realize every girl in the city would have a broken arm by the end of the year, and some would have both arms broken. But every girl likes bread. And most of their husbands and fathers were loath to give them any.

In another stroke of fortune, women were no longer needed to fill out the teams. Men volunteered. Furthermore, they no longer needed a ball, or a rulebook.

The games soon acquired a high rate of casualty, much higher than those in our hero's prior world.

The dilemma posed to the city was that, as barbaric a sight as basketball was, the nobles enjoyed the divertissement. Less men in the city meant more wives for the nobles, though it also meant less men to work caravans, build buildings, and serve tea. However, on further contemplating the matter, more work meant more coordination, which meant more work from the nobles, who were currently content with all of the city's wealth.

They thus chose the option most favorable and time-honored among them: they did nothing, for doing nothing was the luxury most affordable to people with wealth. Yet there was some discomfort in knowing the sisters ate the rival team's bodies afterwards.

The men, the basketball players, did not seem to mind. Men peculiarly feel, or wish to feel, they are equals in all acts of destruction, even when they are participating in their own. In fact, they welcomed it: today they are eager to tell their friends of the scar they acquired, the elbow they broke, or the eyepatch they must wear, and tomorrow they will worry about workers' compensation.

Eventually, the king seized the rights to the game, so as to profit by it. As the inventor, commissioner, and the owner of the only successful team, our hero was rewarded with more debt, on behalf of all the widows and orphans basketball created.

Our hero was distraught at accumulating more debt. He would have to spend five new lives servicing clients to pay off this sum. He made up his mind to end this one and start a new one on a clean slate.

The businesswoman, upon hearing this, had a proposition for him, while eating the bread in his hand. The city's nobles gathered together for weekly auctions. Our hero would be presented with several appraisals collected by the businesswoman, and he would sell himself on the condition that he perish within a year of employment.

A doctor appraised him first. The doctor noted that, regardless of our hero's weight, he was in good health, and thus had a working heart, set of livers, set of lungs, *et cetera*, which would be useful for those in need.

The recruiter appraised him next. He noted that our hero was unusually obedient and diligent, as a result of a decade of indoctrination in primary and secondary school, though he was very stupid. He was not fit for physical labor, but he was able to perform more sophisticated roles, as yes-man and fall guy.

A mage appraised him next. He observed that our hero did not have a scrap of intelligence towards learning magic, but he noted the unusual makeup of our hero's blood that would act as a component for certain rituals and potions.

A cleric appraised him next. He observed that our hero was faithful, but lacked the imagination needed to devote himself entirely to a god. He could make for a good sacrifice, though.

A chef appraised him next. He said, very clearly, though cannibalism was illegal in the city, someone who preferred the taste of human meat over any other's may find him delectable as a result of his adipose tissue.

A madam appraised him next. She noted that our hero was unlikely to hurt or disagree with a person. However, his tastes were fairly vanilla. Thus he would make for a good pet or good sport or, alternatively, a willing donor if an heir was desperately needed.

An artist appraised him next. He noted our hero's drawing skills were fine, but he consistently drew the female body in outrageous proportions and generally drew his subjects in flat angles. This outraged our hero; he and the artist fought on stage; the artist won; and so it was appraised that our hero was no fighter.

Our hero was finally awarded to a man wearing a tabard depicting an eagle with a serpent in its talons, the standard of a notable family. When asked why, this august gentleman with some grey answered: "I intend to take this and other assets I have procured today on my final campaign into the hinterlands." He was most persuaded by the appraisal of our hero's former recruiter, who did not discern any skills except in sketching. "I desire a triptych depicting my last triumph and will use the sketches to commission it. That is how I will honor the terms of expiration; in fact, I think this business will be over within a week." With that, he towed our hero away in chains along with a great many other men.

12

Our hero was drilled in maneuvering in chainmail, caring for and using swords, and changing tactics during battle. He had displayed such ability in all of these that he was often rewarded with longer drills and beatings. As much as he had been looking forward to losing weight, he found himself unable to finish a tenth of each activity, and the soreness from the beatings reduced this to a twentieth. Nevertheless he became popular during training, so much so his fellow soldiers sought him out to effusively praise him for holding them back in every exercise.

The camaraderie and loyalty gained from these days would not last. Not long into the campaign half of the army would resign, by reason of aerial bombardment. Where they were promised medals for honorable conduct and death, they were instead bestowed very large rocks. The distinguished gentleman was surprised his usual strategy of outnumbering the enemy did not work, despite employing it several times during the battle.

However, what distinguishes a fighter from a common man is their persistence. He ordered a retreat through a shallow part of a river, which was not very shallow at all. Horses drowned, the men contracted various diseases, as worm-under-toenail and bloody urination, and the enemy greeted them on the other side with sharp pikes.

The distinguished gentleman reasoned that, as the origin of the diseases came from water, the element opposing was dryness. He therefore moved them to the desert. The army indeed lost all access to water as planned, but they were quickly decimated by the scorching day, the freezing nights, and the giant antlions. They resorted to drinking the dew off the corpses in the morning, and eating the jerky of their fellow comrades in the afternoon.

This paradise did not last long. The enemy waged war on the dunes. The distinguished gentleman deemed this an auspicious battle. The enemy brought forth their artillery, the gentleman his; the enemy brought out their full battalions, the gentleman his; the sun was close to the horizon when the fighting started; by the end of the day thousands of men who surely missed their wives and children and whose names and faces were unknown to their generals lost their lives, for the glory of battle. Best of all, as was honorable, their bodies could not be returned for burial, as battle demanded the most battered, most mangled, most destroyed bodies, each potential temples of human wisdom and knowledge, of its brave soldiers.

When the distinguished gentleman heard that only a hundredth of his army remained, he praised the good news. More death meant more success, and he was happy to touch on the wisdom that he bought them all for cheap. When he found there were only a hundred men left, he cursed his lack of learning in mathematics.

The enemy desired to chase them out of the dunes back into the forests from whence the army came. The distinguished gentleman knew this by the words of every envoy the enemy had sent him whom, because of the rules of war, he systematically tortured and killed, as was common sense. Despite this he had no intention to flee back to the vales and glens he knew so well; he wanted to be rewarded with a bear's pelt by the king, to impress his new favorite mistress. If his hundred had to face the enemy's tens of thousands, so be it; in the worst case, he may be refunded their price by the king, though there would be no pelt to gain.

In the darkest hour, he visited our hero, to see his sketches and to evaluate in what way he would sacrifice his life. Our hero drew our distinguished gentleman, dressed in his ancestral emblems and armor, looking grand and ambitious, with the desert winds blowing his cape gallantly. An outcropping of shimmering blue-black banded rock stood in the background, looking like a man.

The two armies stood face to face. The gentleman's army looked like a beetle surrounded by ants, whose limbs were soon to be wrenched apart by millions of black jaws. Just as the horns of battle were to be blown, massive rocks plummeted upon the enemy army, killing many a man. In the subsequent retreat, the survivors grew very ill, having eaten the diseased bodies of their victims.

The enemy lived on a fertile delta in the desert. The distinguished gentleman's city enjoyed prosperity by plundering them every season. When they fell into despair, they prayed to the old spirits of the desert for protection.

This same guardian was toppled over by half of the gentleman's army, those enormous blue-black rocks crushing its devotees. The gentleman did not plan this out of malice; it was merely very big and about to fall. The plan worked admirably, and he congratulated himself. Unfortunately, as a result of overworking these soldiers, all fifty perished from fatigue. His own wrist too was sore from whipping them. He made the decision to camp at the outskirts of the desert waiting for reinforcements to arrive.

There was an unusually large brood of a certain type of insect this season. Their young would burrow into a victim's ears or genitals, make their way into the intestines, and mate there; by the next season, the victim will burst with their eggs, often suffering excruciating pain throughout. Because nothing could or ever will be done for this type of parasite, the men had to camp for quite a long time.

As they were cut from supply lines, the men drew lots as to who would be eaten first. The men hoped our hero would be drawn first. Fortunately, he drew the second-longest straw. If he had been drawn the longest straw, they would have concluded the uselessness of the exercise and devoured him first. As it happened, the distinguished gentleman drew the longest.

Without dice, they resorted to telling stories to cure their boredom, but very boring people only have boring stories, as the goings-on of their dogs, misadventures with women, things their physician say they should do and refrain from, and meaningless advice concerning money from the wisdom of those who have never had any.

Only the distinguished gentleman, who possessed enough wealth to have leisure, had interesting stories. He told a story of another campaign where he was captured by a lord and taken prisoner; upon finding out his virtues, made him slave; how he outwitted the lord constantly and yet became his most trusted confidante; his sexual activities with every one of the lord's wives and daughters; finally the escape with the lord's loot on the back of a drake, and a lovely lady in each hand. I will leave you to decide, dear reader, whether you believe the man's stories, but the men were greatly impressed by the stories, as they ate their daily allotment of human stew, and the distinguished gentleman concluded that every life is full of misfortune and every man has his day as a slave and as a warrior.

The last part was debated, as the men there had spent all of their lives hitherto as slaves. To which the gentleman reasoned:

"The gods make slaves of men and the gods make nobles of men. I was made noble and you were made slaves. This is a good, just and kind thing they have bestowed on us.

"For you can give a man wealth and access to everything he can see, and he will still be unhappy. Purpose is what drives men. It is your purpose to serve me, and it is my purpose to rule over you. That is why the gods made you strong and brave, while they made me wise, intelligent, wealthy, and good-looking. And because the gods are great, they made my life more worthy and worthwhile than yours, as there are fewer men like me.

"Without this order, there would be no walls, or homes, or swords to defend them. There would not even be a scrap of food to eat. Who would make them unless I gave the order to do so?

"You should thus be happy to be slaves, as the gods have given you a singular purpose in life. Myself, I find I can do so many more things than you can, and I am astounded and confused by their multitude. Oh, if only I were born a slave!"

This was a reasonable argument, and the men went on

happily eating one another and telling stories.

Soon, the distinguished gentleman became ill; he micturated blood and felt pain in his abdomen. He found the dried pupae of the insect aforementioned in his stool.

Because he was wise, he did not tell his men there was in fact a cure for this disease – for if the miserable and many knew of cures, they would know hope and therefore despair – but to acquire this he needed to return to the city.

He thus ordered them to take him to the city. They argued there was no hope in helping a dead man.

He argued that, due to his noble blood, his will needed to be followed by mandate of the gods. They argued that, seeing his noble body was given to death, the gods' mandate was very clear.

He argued that he wished to see his wives and children before he was to die, and won't they take pity on the poor soul? But they would be unable to give that pity if they themselves were to die.

He then argued that their actions amounted to insubordination, and that they would be executed upon their betrayal being found out. The men looked at each other; they asked, Who, among the living by day's end, will tell?; no one raised his hand, except for our hero, and this same hand was slapped down.

Their stomachs then argued that it was the time of the day for food. Because they were honorable men, they respected the lottery and ate the man with the shortest straw. However, it was getting a bit drafty, so they killed the distinguished gentlemen for leather. They roasted the eggs as a snack.

This gave them an idea. They feared revenge by a commander when reinforcements arrived, regardless of the story they told him. A tailor among them who was very skilled in his craft created a costume out of the distinguished gentleman's skin. It happened that our hero was the same height as the gentleman, and the surcoat hid the size of his belly. This is how our hero became a general overnight.

The replacement general, accompanied with several thousand men, greeted our hero, disguised as the distinguished gentleman, cordially. Our hero relayed all the army endured, what the enemy's position and strengths were, and possible ways they could take the delta city. The replacement found the gentleman surprisingly pleasant to speak to, a great deal more intelligible, and open to other's opinions; in short, displaying behavior unbecoming of a noble, but behavior propitious for an upstart like himself who sought to raise in status.

For this reason, the replacement poisoned our hero's food; unfortunately, our hero could not finish the last course. He poisoned our hero's wine; water was good enough for him. He even poisoned a bewitching woman's genitals; but our hero had in mind only one woman.

With our hero's advice, the army made it safely through the desert, past the river, and, unopposed, to the edge of the city, with all several thousand men intact. This was unfortunate, as the replacement sought to put some kind of deficiency or blame on our hero.

On the day the two armies were to face one another, the replacement suggested our hero take charge of the men to bolster their courage. Our hero could not refuse, as his answer was drowned in a chorus of applause.

Thus, saddled on a horse he had never learned to ride, armed with a sword he always failed to swing, he eyed the leader of the opposing force, an immense man bigger than a tree, hair reaching his knees, wielding an axe painted red from the countless foes and widows he had slain.

Before the horns of battle were blown the enemy sent an envoy: it was desired that a duel should settle this ancient argument, whose origin no one remembered. The replacement heartily accepted.

Our hero and the giant squared off. The giant was disappointed our hero was not a lion, whose jaws he enjoyed stretching to their extremes before ripping them apart. He was also disappointed our hero was not a woman, whose limbs he liked to tear apart, after the act of satiating himself upon her. He was also disappointed our hero was not a bear, whose throat he liked to crush as it was screaming its death. In short, this was a very disappointing afternoon, and the giant wished our hero was himself, for that would have been a truly great battle.

Before the duel could begin, our hero excused himself, for the sake of relief.

The sun had come down quite a ways down while our hero was relieving himself.

The giant was much upset at our hero's tardiness as he felt there had to be honor in something. He threw down his arms and stormed into the camp, throwing it inside out searching for the specific pot our hero was squatting over.

Upon finding our hero's food, he ate it; upon finding the wine, he drank it; upon finding the woman, he ravished her, and then scattered her limbs into the winds (she found neither experience pleasant); he then fell to his knees, having taken three helpings of poison. The army cut the giant up into pieces, and then cut the opposing army into ribbons, for their hindquarters were much sore after sitting for so long.

The sack of the city was glorious, the murdering limitless. Children cried over the corpses of their mothers and fathers, grandmothers had their brains spilled for their paltry possessions, and men and women who spent their entire lives perfecting a profession had their stores looted and themselves sold to slavery. The king was so happy with this that the replacement was awarded a bear pelt; the men were so happy to pilfer a few pieces of furniture and clothing that they forgot they would resume their lives of boredom and ignorance, and looked forward to next year's war.

Our hero ran back to the city, having stripped himself of his costume. He encountered the healer, and reported happily that he had no longer any debt, but was sad that he was at a loss for what to do now. The healer did not understand and then left the bottles of his home only to make some gold pieces from some soldiers who needed healing in the war. Out of politeness he asked our hero what it is he truly wanted to do. "I want to be an adventurer," he replied. The healer had once been an adventurer; perhaps our hero would like to join him? Our hero could find no other proposition more agreeable.

15

On the morrow our hero, to cement his reputation as an adventurer, paid the Adventurer's Guild a visit to register himself as one. The adventurers made our hero's initiation a very big ceremony. They all gathered together with food and beer, forbade our hero from having any, unpantsed him, forced him upside, and each and every one spanked him, squeezed his genitals, threw goblets of wine at him, and beat him with sticks. The last part of the ritual involved penetrating his rear, but he had let out some wind so noxious that they could not bear it. As all of these steps were crucial, they could not admit him as a member, but they would try the next day.

When our hero told the healer, he replied the Adventurer's Guild was in name only and merely a hangout for the city's nobles when they were bored. No registration was actually needed to go on an adventure.

He then savagely beat our hero, much worse than the adventurers combined, such that it was hard to hide the wounds. When our hero had breath to speak, he asked him why he was treated this way; the healer replied he could not remember the beating, and drank more.

Though our hero was beaten quite a lot in the new world, more than he was in the old world, he felt deep anger at this beating, so deep it surprised him. When other people beat him, they felt they were above him. Because the healer treated him as an equal and shared pies with him, and even gave him a special armor made of mythril, and because the healer did not recall the beating and thus felt no need to apologize for it, our hero felt it was not justified. Though this anger was quite deep, he merely deposited it, as he did in the former world.

The forests were very active this season. The healer took a request to protect a town far from the city. Griffins had strangely built their nest near it while the townsfolk set up for a festival.

The healer was wily and set up traps consisting of nets. The nets were designed to trap the griffins' wings, so they could not fly away from their slaughter.

Our hero felt this was a good plan and witnessed its execution in the town square. His relaxation allowed the griffins to eat him.

As griffins have no teeth, he dove headfirst, body intact, into the steaming intestines of the griffin, a jet of acid splashing his face. Fortunately the armor withstood the corrosive acid and he climbed his way through.

The griffin destroyed the townspeople's homes, kicked them down, and ripped them apart with its beak. The townspeople cursed that their houses were made of sticks and straw. They then saw a curious sight: the griffin paused, scratched urgently some phantom itch, then began beating and scratching its rump against a tree. When in its agony it chanced to turn around, the townfolk saw our hero's head poking out of its rump.

Our hero recalled he had a knife with him. Upon cutting his way through, the griffin's innards collapsed, and our hero escaped on a tide of blood and fecal matter.

Having come from the griffin's rear, our hero carried the

griffin's scent. He was covered in the pheromones that attracted male griffins, who then swooped down from the sky and stood proudly and erect before our hero. Because the lower half of a griffin is a lion's, our hero stared at a palisade of long thick staves and felt terror.

Fortunately the townsfolk came, armed with swords and spears, and cut down and pierced these spears, spilling their blood onto the ground. This was a great good day for them, for griffin blood was considered crucial for male potency, and they poured it into bathtubs.

This season was often accompanied with the flights of love and in the celebration that evening our hero fell into a conversation with a local girl. They talked; she ignored his replies; because she was a brave girl she undressed him; as she undressed herself he closed his eyes, not believing the greatness of the moment. Strong arms held his back. He opened his eyes. The healer began beating him, for the state of the armor he had given him.

The healer kicked his body black and blue, and the girl returned to the arms of her lover. The bounties of the night seemed endless.

16

Our heroes took a request to rescue a team of researchers in a nearby labyrinth. The labyrinth consisted of old tombs built by the citizens' forebears, containing the history of their civilization and the secrets to magic and mortality. These would be excellent topics for research, however they were primarily concerned with means to add to the king's hoards.

The labyrinth was dark, humid, and full of dust, all attributes our hero disliked. The healer traced the researchers' steps and came across their bodies in a heap.

The healer heard footsteps in the distance. A tribe of goblins had made their home there.

The goblins took no pleasure in the presence of humans and picked up their knives and clubs to protect their children. They surrounded our heroes and shouted angrily. The healer understood that they wanted them to leave, and unrolled a scroll, whose letters erupted into a ball of fire aimed at the goblins. The labyrinth was old and shook, and collapsed. The healer was quick, our hero was not; he fell and plummeted deep into a hole.

The healer reported this situation to the Adventurer's Guild, members of royalty, even the king himself. He went through every personal connection, but none were willing to save our hero, much less thought him worth saving. The labyrinths were designed in strange ways, meant for rituals, and our hero could have fell however many feet into danger. Furthermore, the dust raised from the collapse made the labyrinth unbreathable. The healer hung up his head, drank for several days, and returned home without a shirt or a gold piece, feeling unhappier than when he lost our hero.

However, our hero did survive. The corpses of the goblins and the researchers cushioned his fall.

As he had been in this situation not long ago, he gathered these same corpses, which saved his life, around himself, so he may eat them.

As there was no water, he chose the most attractive of the corpses, opened its mouth, and urinated into it, so he may drink out of it like a goblin goblet of wine. He disliked this method, but a complete lack of flexibility disallowed him from drinking straight from the source.

As there was no exit, and no light, our hero felt his best option was to stay put. However, as a result of his recent adventures, he had begun to realize that doing nothing was not always a viable action, that doing nothing, after all, was doing nothing, and he could not be certain whether anyone was coming to save him.

Thus, out of anxiety, and out of his control, he began passing wind, whose odor came from the corpses. He tried to prevent himself from passing wind, as he felt that doing so expended energy, by cupping his hand over his bottom. Over time the gas filled the hole, and steeped in his own fumes our hero thought.

He conceived of a light novel based on his adventures. The promise to not be a light novelist in this world, that he made himself, would have to be broken. The novel would be concerned with peace and justice, good and evil, of a muscular and impossibly handsome but meek and artistic hero of six feet height, of an impossibly beautiful girl who fell in love with the hero and struggled to find clothing to conceal her large breasts, and of a villain so evil he was willing to destroy the earth that he himself lived on. The twist is that the girl would not be in love with the hero initially, as, despite his muscles and his good looks, he was too meek. Eventually she would see all the virtues in him, and they would consummate, dressed in strawberries and whip cream.

"This is a good idea," our hero thought, breathing in his own wind.

Though the goblins did not enjoy the presence of humans, their widows and children felt something like compassion for our hero, possibly as a result of the recent deaths; they also did not think smelling one's farts was healthy; they were also disturbed by his cackling at his own jokes.

They approached the hole, their arms full of food and drink; they smelled the gas; they died; and they tumbled into the hole; and as the hole was very dark, our hero had none of their food and drink, and ate their bodies, their clothing, and the possessions on their person instead.

The bodies soon piled high enough for him to leave. He found that leaving his own smell made him less creative. He also found that this experience made him gain more weight, not less. He was hoping to acquire abs from starvation.

Our hero was reunited with the healer, who felt the taste of his tears was better than any wine brewed. As a result of the dangers of this adventure, and our hero's indigestion, they took a reprieve from adventuring. This would have made our hero happy if the indigestion were not so painful.

Finally, after many hours over the pot, our hero pushed it out: a brooch whose jewel shone a brilliant complex green.

He had pushed out many things, and would push out many things, as pieces of dresses, toys, canes and baby teeth, though this was the most prominent thing.

17

Upon learning our hero had a brooch to sell, the businesswoman offered to sell it for him.

When the brooch was discovered to have belonged to goblins, despite its beauty, it did not sell for much. The many appraisals and models she acquired to increase its value helped its price little.

Our heroes sought respite from their task and walked around the city, finding a parade in their path.

The king asked the healer if any treasures were found from our heroes' last adventure. The healer, dissatisfied with the king's reaction to our hero's danger, replied that he, in fact, did: he found a set of magical clothing.

The healer held it up. The king professed to see nothing. The healer asserted they were invisible clothing, woven by elves. The king put them on. He felt neither warmth from the cold nor comfort from the wind. The healer asserted that elves had a great deal of veneration for nature, and felt that the best clothing argued for an intimate connection with that same nature. Believe me, the healer said, in-between inhalations of his flask, I once knew many elves.

The king finally asked, Is this clothing very expensive? To which the healer responded, Yes, the more threadbare, the more expensive.

The king thus demanded a ceremony to celebrate his acquisition of these very expensive clothes. He ordered trumpet-players to trumpet, drummers to drum, and beautiful women to be beautiful. He paraded his invisible but very expensive clothing to all the noblemen and noblewomen first. Most of the noblewomen had already seen him naked, and most of the noblemen had seen there was nothing to him, and so they had very diminished reactions.

He then paraded himself to the commoners, who were surprised that the king would allow himself to be seen in such a state, but not very surprised to see he possessed nothing impressive underneath his usual attire. A child remarked that the king was not wearing anything; this child was considered very stupid; he was stupid not because he was incorrect about the king's true state, but that he even cared in the first place. For kings are kings because they are most forgiven for their follies.

The king ordered the child to be executed. The businesswoman, who found little disagreeable in the king, in fact had said his majesty looked splendid today, inquired after the nature of the king's clothing. The king reiterated what the healer had told him. So the clothing had no weight? Yes, the king affirmed. The clothing could not be felt? Yes, the king affirmed. But the clothing was very expensive? Yes, the king affirmed, worth more than my palace.

Seeing the king was growing tired of these philosophical discursions, the businesswoman suggested that, instead of the very righteous execution of this child, he should instead be sold to the king, to be the bearer of this very delicate piece of clothing. Because the clothes were not heavy, a child could hold them; because the clothes were delicate, only a delicate child could handle them; and because the clothes were very expensive, only a child possessed the innocence not to steal them. And, because the clothes were very expensive, its bearer too needed to be paid great expenses, otherwise this whole thing just didn't make any sense.

The king agreed with all of these. The businesswoman had one more thing to added: a king needs a scepter as a symbol of his power, and she had a scepter to sell.

These events gave the businesswoman a very good idea.

The businesswoman rented an auction room and invited prospective buyers of jewelry for an event. Entering, they found a large goose on center stage, secretly our hero in disguise. This was the magic gold-laying goose. To add to the deception, she placed an even larger goose behind the goose, the very mother who laid the golden egg that birthed the goose who laid golden eggs. To quell any further doubts, the businesswoman supplied the resumés of both goose, which she herself wrote. The goose was very easy to hire as she refused to lay eggs of late due to the grief from losing her newborn.

Our hero would lay an egg from his rear, from which would hatch the brooch. Bidding would begin, and already it earned the highest bids ever placed in an auction in the city. At the end, the businesswoman would declare the winner and promise to distribute the awards after the show. Then she turned the stage around, allowing the goose some solitude and peace to lay another egg. In this moment of darkness she inlaid another cheap gem on the brooch, placed the brooch back in the egg, which was placed back into our hero's rear, turned the stage facing the audience again, and began bidding. The businesswoman was not sure how she would hide the wealth nor how she could spend it; but she felt equipped to handle this in due time.

The longness of the show troubled the giant goose. She stood and walked across the stage. The businesswoman thought she was getting a drink of water. Instead, she squatted over our hero and introduced him to her rear, as she dearly missed the gosling she had birthed.

Ever the professional, the businesswoman continued the auction with a wrinkle: she would offer up next the gold-laying goose. Only true royalty could have made the bids that were offered. During this time, the businesswoman held our hero's legs down, so that at least his stomach was still showing; anything less, and he would have suffocated inside of the giant goose.

The final bid was made, and this could have been honored. She sold our hero to the princess, took the gold pieces from the other auctioneers, and fled the city for a long time. The former felt nothing could be done for the depressed goose except to kill, cook and eat her, which was the only consolation for the nobles who lost much money that day.

18

Though the king had many daughters, the princess was the strangest among them, as a result of being the eldest and thus conferred the most privileges. Having never married, her castle was visited by many men who were struck by her beauty. Though these going-ons were troublesome to her father, who had to dispose of several of them, he felt his daughter's leisure was healthy, as he thought that a woman's value lied in her beauty and she was given many chances to exercise it.

The king was, so it is said, descended from a god. Therefore his children, particularly the princess, dispensed of justice. Their words were wise because their word was sole.

Thus, upon finding our hero was not a gold-laying goose, she judged the whole misunderstanding forgivable, so long as our hero could retrieve for her a jackalope as a pet. Our hero readily accepted.

However, jackalopes did not exist.

Our hero and the healer traveled deep into the forest, which had taken a sinister air as of late. Since the massacre of griffins, several citizens had been slain in this dense, untameable realm of trees. This was not unusual during the season – beside the heightened activity, the fluttering of love and foraging for food after a long frost, and much more inebriation – but the frequency and brutality of the attacks were notable.

They had set up nets under the dark shade and caught a

female deer and a male rabbit. The healer possessed a potion. He tasked himself with smearing the potion on the rabbit's genitals, while our hero was tasked with the doe. This is what a woman's genitals look like, our hero thought. Upon setting the deer and rabbit down, they looked upon one another and, seized with passion, mated.

Gestations of this type could only complete under the guidance of the god of the forest. The healer had some of the forest god's hair; in the sunlight, they shimmered golden and bright. He grafted these hairs onto his finger, which swelled twice its size. Our hero shivered, as he felt something dark and unholy had been done.

The healer drew his finger over the doe's belly, which swelled large and round. Shrieks of agony were uttered by the doe, and the cries of brood came from her gravid belly. The healer severed the rabbit's head and poured its blood over the doe's womb. The jackalope burst from its mother's womb, using the horns to carve through the flesh. The healer swaddled the jackalope with cloth.

The healer heard the dead leaves rustle. He told our hero to hide. They separated, the healer covering the newborn's mouth gently but firmly.

Coming from the thicket was a man with the face and claws of a wolf. The wolf man, upon coming across the bodies of the rabbit and doe, cried, devoured them whole, and searched for their assailants. As the healer predicted, the smell of blood overwhelmed the wolf man's senses. He would leave upon finding no one.

Unfortunately, our hero let out wind.

The wol fman, smelling the wind, pounced across the forest

floor and bit our hero once. The shout of the healer surprised him, as well as the mewling of the illicit brood. He turned tail to pursue the healer, leaving our hero to walk alone, dizzy, on all fours.

19

Our hero made his way back to the city in this hot, confused state. He caught a glimpse of a lovely woman walking out at night and moved toward her so that she might help him relieve his intense heat.

Unfortunately, having pinned her to the ground, he found a member of his was hidden in a stump of flesh. He scratched, bit at where his manhood should have been, but it would not come out. He whined.

The woman owned a dam. This loyal dam, though frightened, barked at our hero in hopes she could successfully intimidate him. At this bitch our hero's manhood presented itself.

Fortunately for our hero, soldiers arrived to stop him before he committed to the act. Unfortunately, they took out their hammers. The woman, feeling pity for our hero, invented the lie that this very ugly, very fat dog was hers and he became far too excited for his own good. Disappointed they were unable to sup on dog that afternoon, the soldiers dispersed.

The woman, despite her act of mercy, was understandably upset. She passed our hero over to her grandmother, who was lonely in her advanced years and required a companion for her failing eyesight.

The grandmother was the kindest woman in the city; for the act of relieving himself on her carpet, she merely had him beaten. However, she had the unusual habit every evening of sitting down on her favorite chair, removing her dress, and smearing her groin with peanut butter. In this state our hero loved peanut butter, and thus licked every inch of it off the grandmother. This perhaps was our hero's worst experience in the new world thus far.

Yet these incidents did not diminish his enjoyment for life, and indeed he considered this a good life. He did not do much thinking and little expectations were burdened on him. He was learning how to relieve himself properly. The only blemish, beside the grandmother's unusual habit, was the mailman. Though he frequently had no mail to deliver – indeed, the grandmother's children never wrote her – he came by, beat our hero, and then went to have his fun with the neighbor's wife. Once he tried to poke out one of our hero's eyes with a knife. Our hero did not mind losing control of his intelligence nor his agency, but he minded his anger.

The mailman stopped by, intending to take our hero's eyes truly. The neighbor's wife recently refused him his fun, as a result of being beaten black and blue for it, and he sought to satisfy himself in other ways.

As he grabbed the door's handle, our hero leapt and bit him on the wrist, such that his teeth met. This morning our hero whined to the grandmother, so she left the door slightly ajar.

The mailman dropped the knife, as our hero bit his stabbing hand. Our hero clenched the knife between his jaws and cut one of the mailman's eyes. This set the mailman running.

He cried for help, anyone's help. A muscled individual approached him. He did not recognize him as the husband of the neighbor's wife.

The muscled man held the mailman down as our hero ravaged his face, until he was finally unrecognizable. The muscled man and our hero high-fived.

He saw the woman he had attacked, the granddaughter of the grandmother.

The woman stepped back, covered her mouth to scream, and held her skirt down. To our hero's surprise, however, she moved closer to him, pet him, and then, with face flushed, began kissing him ear to ear. Clearly he had made an impression on her.

The healer collared our hero. To restore our hero's condition, a certain potion would have to be administered through a catheter.

20

The king allowed adventurers in the dungeon built beneath his castle. All the treasures, dangers and revelations were for the public's taking.

The king had an obsession with his lineage, particularly concerning an ancestor who was purportedly a god. Though he often cited this fact, he had never been able to prove it. He held hope that the labyrinth beneath his familial land possessed the proof of this connection. He also laid claim to a certain proportion of any treasure found, as he of late became much jealous of a certain noble, the replacement.

The local Adventurer's Guild gathered to elect a leader for this expedition. They proposed an election between the two most senior adventurers. One had lost his mind, and the other was made crippled and incontinent by a chimera. Both of their faces sagged, both ate food mushed, and both only remembered where the bathroom was.

On the day of the election, both deceased. Their sons were nominated, neither of whom had experience as adventurers. They made grand promises about the things that were to be discovered and grand lies concerning their method of achieving success. These arguments were met with cool reception. The nominees then began slandering the other, calling the other impotent, lame, stupid, and traitors to the Adventurer's Guild. This was met with far greater enthusiasm, for they both were impotent, lame, and stupid, but they were the only candidates available for voting. The guild was so inflamed by their speeches, and so moved by the fact that both candidates were unworthy, that both were assassinated by the end of the week.

After many speeches where both sides accused the other of stirring violence for their own gain, two new nominees were named. Not only did the slander intensify, the nominees found they were capable of doing every kind of harm to their constituents, as taking their wealth and their wives, and slaying anyone they did not like, not based on their own merit, but on their opponents' lack of merit, which, as we recall, was half a truth and half an invention. As both parties were desperate to defeat the other, they gave their candidate access to more and more power, which each believed to be granted by their own merit rather than the mob, and so both were felled in a duel, which they thought they could win, though neither knew how to use swords.

Two new nominees were named. These same two promptly left town the same night, as they desired to live, and they did not enjoy making speeches.

Now no one wanted to be leader, and people were forced to accept nominations, and consequently people were forced to excuse themselves from running, as choking on a meal, being kicked by a horse, slipping in a bathtub. One very fortunate man had won an election, a man who deserved to be leader for his accomplishments yet was passed up for louder men, stood up to the applause, sat down, and died on that very seat, for reasons unknown to this day.

Finally our hero and the healer nominated themselves. This was long after the adventurers, who consisted only of nobles, began nominating their horses, dogs, and cats, so the precedent had been set. The healer made many good arguments, as filling the dungeon with air, using salamanders to light the way, and had many opinions on armaments and tools. The audience, however, preferred our hero, who said very little and thus had little to scrutinize. They also empathized with him more, as they too were not adventurers. Our hero won by a landslide, and the healer accepted a role as his advisor, whose duty involved beating the sense into our hero occasionally.

21

The healer recommended a soldier, a mage, and a linguist to add to their team. They chose the finest soldier, a scarred man who distinguished himself in the most recent war by receiving the most spears inside his body. They chose the finest mage, a woman who studied in a renowned college some cities away. They chose the best linguist, the businesswoman who had no formal training but self-taught herself several languages from the royal library, whose books she stole. With himself and our hero, they made a team of five. He then divided the other adventurers into teams of five, decided arbitrarily what were the best talents of whom, and believed between half to a tenth of them would live through the ordeal.

After a long ceremony, in which the king called them all brave, wise adventurers and exhorted them to uncover the mysteries of the dungeon, our heroes descended. They dispatched living slimes and giant rodents, disarmed traps, and deciphered some of the hieroglyphics, which described a deity who the king possibly originated from. The other adventurers quickly deceased from the lack of oxygen their torches siphoned. The healer had a lantern with a living fire sprite which, being magical, did not require material.

They encountered a large sacrificial chamber painted in dried blood. The skeletons of victims were tied to the chairs there. The deciphered text showed that, every year, seven men and seven women were sacrificed to the minotaur every seventy seven years. The upper part of the minotaur that was a bull's fed on the flesh of the men. The lower half of the minotaur that was a man's required the flesh of the women. Lurking in the darkness the minotaur bellowed, much upset at the absence of sacrifices in however many centuries.

It was here the mage revealed she knew only magic theory, and little in the way of application. She could attest that the universe was made of four elements, and that magic consisted of manipulating these elements using catalysts, but she hardly produced a fireball. The healer did not tell her even this theory was wrong. Upon the minotaur's entrance, its beard caked with blood, the soldier allowed himself to be gored by the minotaur, for standing in the line of fire was all he knew to do. Unfortunately, the beast had little to do with one body.

Finding none of their arms worked, our heroes fled into the labyrinth, each becoming lost in the endlessly branching paths. The minotaur followed the red of the mage's dress, and her screams intermixed with the minotaur's bellows echoed throughout the maze. After some time groping in the darkness, our heroes met again and debated on what to do. It was possible the minotaur was satiated on the mage and the soldier, but they could not plan on this circumstance. The healer knew no magic that could directly harm anyone. The businesswoman could rely on only one type of magic.

The minotaur dragged the mage in the dirt, desiring to save her for later. He made his way to the soldier's corpse. It was then the healer struck him in the head with his staff. Rather than feeling pain, he felt the speed and quality of his thoughts grow, he felt new concepts and emotions surge into him, in short, he felt enlightened. His intelligence increased, the businesswoman presented the argument the life he was leading was a waste – after all, he had spent however many centuries in this dungeon and was not getting any younger – and that to lead a truly virtuous life he needed to become a pacifist, a vegetarian, and a husband to this young woman whom he had lied with. He had no previous exposure to ethics and philosophy, he was baffled enough by his developing conscience to agree. Thus the college graduate became a woman, and the minotaur a thinker, and both were now wedded.

22

The businesswoman taught the minotaur their language, and his wife taught him magical theory. The minotaur learned skills so quickly it seemed everyone should be hit on the head at least once.

The businesswoman understood from the dungeon's text that the minotaur originated from the forest god's coupling with a human woman. The minotaur was upset to not remember the mother he once had, but he was reconciled to know that with this knowledge, or lack of knowledge, he was recently wedded and needed no other woman. Our hero was slightly envious of the minotaur. The healer continued medicating himself with alcohol.

Our hero and the healer slayed several giant rats, which were the offspring of giants and rats, and they feasted for the evening. The healer showed how to clean the rats' organs of disease, set up a fire, and roast the innards with some fungi harvested in the dungeons. The businesswoman figured only a person who drank as excessively as the healer knew how to eat things scrounging a cellar floor. They slept in makeshift beds, and when they awoke they were surrounded by goblins, who took them to their village.

The goblin chief assured them they had no ill intent. The goblins had long ago retreated from the sunlight, fleeing from the humans' malice. They dug tunnels to other underground labyrinths and built settlements there. Recently one of these tunnels collapsed, and they were unsure what happened to their brothers, sisters, nephews and nieces on the other side and hoped our heroes knew. They all confessed not to know, and continued polite, engaging conversation, exchanging quite a bit of information on the dungeon.

For example, the dungeon was host to a great dragon and a river of slime. The river was once considered the origin of all life in the forest. Our hero excused the group to relieve himself.

A goblin led him to a patch of dirt, dug a hole and instructed him to relieve himself in the hole. Our hero did so. In the process of covering the hole, the goblin found a brooch with his aunt's signature inscribed on it. This aunt had migrated to the lost colony. The goblin held onto this brooch and informed the chief, who remained silent until dinner.

Before they could sup on a pot of stew, the chief asked if his guests recognized the brooch. The businesswoman replied that it would have a fetching price at auction. This was sufficient proof to the goblins who promptly pointed their spears at our heroes.

Fortunately the soldier, who they hitherto thought deceased, leapt in front of them, received the spears, and died, as valor dictated. The minotaur refused to direct a fireball at the goblins, as he considered himself a good man. The healer instructed him to fire overhead, which he complied with. The awesome fireball roared from his staff, illuminating the room with golden light and struck the ceiling which collapsed into rock. The goblins were trapped in their dung heap.

Our heroes, satisfied with their success, took a different route back to the village to eat the villagers' food and sleep in their beds. The couple took the goblins' clothing for their future children, the businesswoman took jewelry from the funeral ashes, and our hero took the goblin chief's staff. An orb of pure azure, it contained complex lines that made the mind wandered and mirrored the endless variation of the universe. Our hero expressed the desire to learn magic, but the healer was becoming distressed at the stock of liquor running out.

23

The healer became sick without drink. He profusely sweated, hallucinated, and was unable to move on his own. Our heroes did not realize how necessary he was until our hero cooked breakfast. Raw in parts, bland in others, the mage became ill after ingesting it. She too had to be carried to the river of slime.

The living slime is all of one quantity. It only consists plasma, which possesses digestive acids, and the eggs themselves contained no DNA but were programmed to copy the host's DNA perfectly. The living slime thus is a single-purposed and selfish creature, whose sole purpose involved no play and only reproduction.

Our hero brought out a knife to cut the slime and gather their gelatinous material to eat. The soldier, whom our heroes believed deceased, upon seeing a sharp edge, threw himself onto the knife, dying for the sake of his comrades and his honor.

Our heroes decided to use the soldier's body as a raft, and though this river was difficult to paddle through with makeshift paddles they made substantial progress. They saw a mighty Cerberus at the other side of the river. The sight of this fearsome beast caused our hero to faint and fall into the slime.

The slime immediately rushed into every entrance of his; they filled the canals of his ear; they ran into the room of his lungs; they avoided the bowels; they poured into the urethra and coursed through the testes. He fainted from the pain.

The businesswoman and the minotaur fished our hero out of the river. Upon him surfacing, they found him a bigger man, particularly in the abdominal region. Our hero touched his swollen belly with his hands and felt a kick. He was pregnant with a child.

However, he was incorrect. He was pregnant with hundreds of children. They were growing very quickly and his stomach bulged, nearly unable to contain them. He hardly noticed the pain, however, from the nausea and a newfound desire for pickles and peanut butter.

The businesswoman and the minotaur deliberated quickly. The minotaur raised the knife; our hero shrank from it. This was a wise decision from our hero as, despite his acquired intelligence, the minotaur was no surgeon.

They reasoned birth could come out of the mouth, the urethra or the anus. Our hero did not think children coming out of his member was a good idea.

Our heroes patted our hero's stomach rigorously, ensuring he had the proper circulation. Our hero made a retching sound, then burped; one baby came out. He groaned, and wind was heard; a second baby came out. Through this process, of the businesswoman guiding lumps to the mouth, and the minotaur through the anus, alternating them, a great many children were born, cooing and crying.

The minotaur, who had acquired a brain not long ago, concluded he could not be compelled to have children with the mage. The businesswoman was almost there in terms of belief as well, and in terms of throwing up.

The children were near identical to him: they shared his

eyes and hair color and possessed the same face. These traits did not endear them to our hero, and in fact he felt disappointed they were predisposed to grow up just like him, in consideration of the fact that he had been put into a position of giving birth to a hundred babies. To his fortune, the businesswoman and the minotaur, both of wide-ranging philosophies, reasoned that they were slime and not human children, and thus it did not matter how they reflected on him and what happened to them. He felt these arguments were compelling.

Upon reaching the other end of the bank our heroes fed the Cerberus infants until it slumbered. They then made infant sandwiches and infant soup to eat. Seeing there were still too many remaining, they had the infants pull sleds and trigger traps involving boulders and flaming spikes. When they were bored, they played kickball and tetherball.

24

The mausoleum was guarded by a ferocious sphinx who presented her three riddles. If they failed to answer them, she would eat them. Our heroes assured her the infants were sincere in their answering.

The sphinx having perished from eating poisoned infants, our heroes entered the tomb, to unfortunately be separated by living walls. Our hero, carrying the healer delirious with pain, tried everything in his power to move the obstacles, but finally felt the strength leave him from intense thirst. As he had suffered from deprivation before, he felt twice as much fear, and felt twice as powerless. He sat, contemplating that this was the doom of himself and the healer.

From the darkness shuffled the immortal bodies of kings past. Embalmed alive using arcane sorceries, they lived eternally but were very bored of long living quite early into it. The flame in their eyes went out and the spark of intelligence left their heads. They moved toward our hero with the urges that sustained them while living. Our hero tried to resist, but strengthened by dark magic they pinned him, moved his head to their organs, and satisfied themselves as they would with their mistresses in the past life. Came flooding in were happy memories of themselves and their concubines that they relieved every last drop of life into the act, and finally exited this life to the thereafter, if any existed for them. In-between kings, our hero took every second liquid and poured it into the healer's mouth.

Having relieved his thirst by several lineages of scions, he gathered his strength and found the kings had came from a door dim in the darkness of the tomb. Two dwarves greeted him as they rested on their anvils. They had been buried with the kings as a reward for their skillful work, and found the glory of the afterlife quite stale. Our hero had never seen a dwarf before and supposed their race rare. The dwarf replied that his father and his grandfather had lived in the mountains, forging ingenious tools, and he himself came to the city for work when times were difficult. As for the other, he was a very short man.

The dwarf and the dwarf led our hero to the treasure. In this room was all of the kings' glorious treasure, things they cherished in life, as weapons, armor and ornaments. Loyal in this life and loyal in their death, the living walls, which the kings kept as pets, guarded the treasure as our heroes approached it.

The healer's nose twitched. He leapt from our hero's shoulders and, in an incredible show of strength, crushed the walls between his fingers. Here too were barrel racks of vintage wine.

As the other heroes had arrived, they decided to rest, eat, and take as much loot as possible. Fully armed, even the remaining infants, they felt prepared to face the dragon and were thus in a cheerful mood. They even found jollity by the healer's drunken ramblings. As he was far more inebriated than he had been used to, and very gay as a result of long suffering, he invented an amusing yarn that he had once lived in another world, been married there with a child, and had deceased in an untimely fashion only to return to live in this world as an adventurer. His life, in his words, was a neverending nightmare originating from a devil in disguise as

a goddess, and most horrible was his having experienced
loss twice in the form of an adventuring party that had
become a second family to him. Indeed nothing could ruin our
heroes' hopes for the future.

25

The dragon made its residence in the church at the lowest level of the dungeon. She invited our heroes cordially from the dark and began a civil conversation with them. There was no more treasure in this church, beyond relics that were useless to her and the immense deer statue the congregation once worshipped, and indeed she craved no treasure. She simply sought quiet here as she had recently just left a lover.

They conversed on the secret of the dungeon. "The current king has no lineage traced to the builders of this mausoleum." In fact, our hero was the true descendant of the scions buried here, as could be detected by the scent of his blood. There was a special make to his flesh that was of divine origin.

As the dragon was proud, our heroes offered to massage her muscles and polish her scales. They asked frequent questions about her former lover. If they weren't rude for asking, they inquired whether the bump in her stomach was a few too many wargs or something else. For the businesswoman and the healer had decided beforehand to slay the dragon and sell her scales for a fortune.

They convinced the dragon she was gravid and, further, she was not equipped to take care of a hatchling. For the dungeon was only a temporary residence, and she lacked any hunting ability even for herself as a result of being provided for by her lover. They suggested an operation to remove the to-be dragon, to which she agreed. They sent a team of infants through the dragon's stomach to push the premature egg out, where it would perish of exposure. Our heroes then noted that her rear had contracted too much. The dragon-slaying blade was required to open her stomach, which would then be sewn shut. They gave her many barrels of wine as a sedative and assured her many dragons found this type of scar attractive.

They found, to their surprise, an actual egg. Upon seeing her beautiful egg, red-banded with specks of gold, she decided now to keep it. She then realized our heroes had no intentions of aiding her and, with the newborn fury of a mother, filled the entire church with flames, burning down the deer. Our heroes' metal armor would have melted, had the soldier, whom our heroes believed deceased, not leapt in front of them, protecting them from the fire and becoming ash as the prize of becoming a martyr.

In the bath of fire and smoke, they smelled a pleasant aroma. This aroma did come not from the soldier, but from the dragon's ribs, for the flames had spilled from her wounds. These flames were not hot enough to dry the tears from her eyes from not knowing the true value of life until now. These tears, as it turned out, sold plenty on the market.

They dined on the dragon's ribs, which were very tender and given a nuanced flavor from the wine. The remnants of the Adventurer's Guild arrived and offered to haul the loot up. Our heroes victoriously made their ascent out.

The king was thankful for all this ancient art and treasure, but feigned disinterest at the true history. He planned for our heroes' assassinations. However, the adventurers opened the goblins' dung heap, unleashing the smell of many defecations, made more potent by the anxiety of being trapped and dying. This smell overwhelmed the castle and killed the king through shock.

By purchasing the remaining infants and bathing in their blood, the replacement was able to convince the city he possessed royal blood and thus became king. He was not pleased by the present state of the king's castle, and ordered a new one built by seizing all the loot the adventurers had found. As it happened, the businesswoman was happily out of the city when the seizure occurred and claimed bandits stole all of her wealth.

Our heroes mourned the soldier's glorious and very virtuous death. The dwarves put themselves to work, and created bad tools for twice the price, catering to their audience's tastes. The mage and the minotaur wed, and their wedding feast consisted of rat skewers, dragon pie and slime pudding. The soldier toasted them, though the groom had slain him. Our hero hid the egg in his rear and continued holding it tightly to himself every evening.

26

Our hero and the healer were invited to a party held by the three sisters. The eldest sister confirmed wine would be had at the party. They agreed to gift their hosts with a bouquet of flowers. Upon arriving, the sisters were pleased by the gift, threw the flowers on the floor, proceeded to wipe themselves with the wrapping paper, then threw the smeared paper also on the floor.

It became very clear that hygiene was of some concern and of no concern to the sisters upon entering the house. The guests, which consisted of deer, boars, rabbits, and monkeys, relieved themselves on the floor. These were the sisters' relatives. They made fun by catching the others' feces, brutalizing the other, and eating the offals the sisters provided as snacks. Our heroes sat, avoided eye contact with the other guests, and determined individually when would be the best time to leave.

The sisters stripped themselves of their clothes, revealing their statuesque bodies. This caught our hero's attention. The healer continued draining whiskey.

The horses then mounted the sisters. The sisters mounted monkeys, the monkeys mounted bears, the bears mounted rabbits, and the rabbits mounted boars, and the house was overcome by grunting, and the house became very sticky and wet.

The youngest sister took our hero by the hand, inducing him to follow her and her beautiful body. The healer refused, for he knew the magic word "No". The sister stripped our hero

83

of his clothes and handled his genitals, lifting a certain member up. She then directed our hero towards a doe, who had kicked the dishes off of a table and pointed her genitals in our hero's direction. The room had become very hot and he felt himself sweating profusely. Our hero closed his eyes and smelled the doe's scent, which was of damp leaves. He felt the warmth of the doe's body. Behind him were the sister's strong hands and round thighs thrusting into his, and in front of him were the doe's thighs into which his were thrusting. He wished to cry; then there was release. The bears, chickens, wolves felt pleasure, he saw none in the back of his eyelids.

When he opened his eyes, the activity paused. A beautiful white buck had entered the room, whom the family greeted with hoarse shouting. The buck walked around the room and did not distinguish between what were food, what were body fluids, and what were his children as he ate. He then spat blood. Indeed, everyone in the house, including the sisters, began spitting blood, except for our hero and the healer who took his protege by the hand and led him out of the massacre.

It was difficult for our hero to understand that the forest creatures had contempt for humans for centuries, planned a massacre, and that the white buck was their patriarch and deity. Our hero viewed these creatures as worthy of sympathy. The healer did not, which was why he poisoned them.

A mighty shriek was heard throughout the immense forest, reaching the city. Women miscarried, healthy men collapsed, and the sick and weak died. Had the healer investigated this, he would have recalled that the citizens could trace their lineage to this same god.

A shimmering white overtook the evening sky. The white buck had grown in size, topping the trees and hiding the moon behind his head.

The healer groaned.

27

The white buck raised his hooves and brought them down onto the king's castle, causing thunder and earthquakes. The castle erupted in a plume of stench, covering the kingdom and the forests with the abdominal smell that accumulated so much over time it was like a deity itself. The god of the forest was stunned and our hero and the healer pinched their noses. This gave the healer time to find his lantern and awaken the fire spirit in it, who in reality was a god of fire he had trapped in the desert.

The god, released, ascended into the heavens as a raging pillar of fire. It possessed no intelligence, as gods are thought to have; its only power was to sustain itself, which it did by setting the forests ablaze and feeding on the god of the forest, who cried, shook in pain, and yet could not defend itself from flame incarnate. The ashes of the forest were caught in an immense dust storm, the lands surrounding the city became desert, and millions of creatures, who lost their homes, family and friends in an instant, prayed helplessly to their god to grant them succor. The buck grew the scales of a salamander, he covered his body in mucus, he became a fish and threw himself into the ocean, but the god of flame fed and fed, for he was a concept and not a reality.

The god of the forest however was not entirely at a loss. The intense heat brought up thunderstorms. The rain cooled the lands and diminished the flames, and the god of fire scampered off as but an ember.

Unfortunately, the rain was on the power of the healer, who

invoked his own deity, the source of all of his awesome powers. The mother of light cleaved the heavens, leaving a ray of white light between the parted thunderclouds. The forest god split in twain, and his corpse fell as tatters onto the ground, struggling to become whole once more. The forest creatures, who felt their lineage more deeply than the sons of man, raised their voices to the heavens and cried for the loss of their father and guardian. Without him, their children and their children's children will forget their origin, and therefore their power, and they all will fade into the dust of time, to be forgotten and trampled by the sons of man.

This was good to the healer's god, for it originated from man's genius. It promoted only man's cause so that all lands would be conquered by his seed and the world would be for his eyes only. The world will be so altered by man's genius that it will be unrecognizable, and this would be a good world, so this god supposed.

The healer did not care one jot about this. These gods were only a convenience to him. He revealed that, as our hero died and was reborn into this world, he also had been invited to be reborn, along with other adventurers, to defeat the demon lords. But the demon lords could not be defeated, indeed no adventurer could defeat them, and he remained imprisoned in this world alone without any meaning to his life except to fend off its decay.

Our hero could hardly contain this, the deaths, and, most of all, the dissolution of trust between himself and the healer. Thus he beat him. He slapped, punched, kick the healer until bruises colored his face, until blood trickled down his eyes, until his own hands were sore and could do no more beating. He felt no happier at the end of it. The healer did not defend himself, and at beating's end departed to drain the nearest bottle of liquor.

28

Our hero tied a rope to a tree and formed a noose out of it. The rope snapped when he put his neck into it.

He saw a knife on the ground and made to cut his own belly open. Unfortunately, the blade was too dull.

He threw himself into a river, but he never fully sank to the bottom.

He tried to set himself on fire with a torch, but his skin was too damp.

He tried to drink himself to death, but he could not steady his hand to drink more wine.

In the morning his clothes dried. He again tried to throw himself into the fire, but the fire was not hot enough.

He insulted and attacked several men on the street, hoping to attract their ire, but they were too upset to retaliate, as their wives had recently miscarried.

He provoked animals, but they were grieving from the loss of their home.

He threw himself onto a rack of swords, but they never pierced his skin.

He ate poison, but only received incontinence.

He sold himself to the army, but there were no wars. As both cities were now deserts, the two cities, having a similarity, reconciled.

He beat himself with a hammer, but he lacked the strength

to crack his skull.

His face broken, his mouth missing a few teeth, he wondered why he was left to live, and he wept in despair.

A bird alighted on his shoulder, bearing a message tied to its foot. The message was from the goddess. She wanted to meet him.

Our hero ran to the healer's home, which was empty. He stole some of the healer's best clothing and sprinted to the bar she would be.

She was somehow even more beautiful from the day he met her. Her skin was white as snow and her breasts were like babies swaddled in cloth.

Some men asked if she minded their sitting with her. She replied that she minded. When they disregarded her, they vanished. No trace of them remained; they simply vanished. No one wanted to sit with her.

Our hero asked if she minded whether he sat with her. She did not. He sat down.

Our hero asked how she has been.

She blinked. "It always is.

"How are you?"

Our hero was doing well.

The goddess was happy to hear this.

A waitress came by and asked what they required. The goddess did not eat, so our hero ordered pie.

"Why do you want the demon lords defeated so badly?"

She blinked. "I do not want them so.

"I guide adventurers so that they are so. That is all.

"If you are asking why my creators wanted it so, I can only speculate. I assume the demon lords destabilize the balance of the worlds. As to what the balance is for, I do not know.

"This world is also linked to your former world, so if events continue as they do now, both worlds may be destroyed.

"I recall I explained this to you when we first met."

Our hero simply forgot.

He then asked about the healer. The goddess recalled him, as well as several other adventurers who were close to defeating the demon lords. But they, alas, could not. They were perhaps the most successful group in a millennium, but, she surmised, "I can not see this world lasting another decade."

Our hero asked who she was.

"I am not a god as other beings in this world are called gods. They are concepts given shape. I am merely a guide between worlds.

"I must be going now. Forgive me if I cannot help you. I am not given much these days."

Our hero was simply glad to see her again and asked if she liked anything in this world. She simply responded, "Flowers, I suppose." She gave our hero one last smile, and then evaporated into beads of light.

29

Our hero read the note on the healer's table he had ignored. The healer left for other lands and left the house to our hero.

Our hero made a resolution, and sought to keep it. He started a garden in the healer's former house. He gave up adventuring. He grew lentils as his main diet. He grew tomatoes, whose cool flesh he would eat in the summer. He grew carrots, which were savory. He grew onions, which would go in soup. He grew fennel, which gave flavor.

Everyone contributed to our hero's garden. The mage and her husband tended crops. The recruiter knew some recipes. The businesswoman bought new seeds. The soldier guarded the garden with his life. The bitch watched it. The prosecutor looked away. The dwarves crafted tools. The doe provided fertilizer. The manpig, much in love with our hero, brought the workers refreshment. The grandmother baked pies. The replacement did not tax it. The werewolf did not take vengeance. The sisters, who survived the poison and held little grudges, as animals often did not, plowed like oxen. Though he had no success in growing flowers, they made a wonderful garden, and in the city where people often ate sawdust with their beer they loved the products. Our hero, after many perilous adventurers, finally had a happy life, and he felt in harmony with the people he could call friends.

It is unfortunate life is not so simple.

The garden was so beloved that it only attracted more and more admirers. Though the sisters were stronger than ten men, our hero asked the recruiter for more hands to help him sow seeds and reap their products. Rather than purchasing the freedom of these people, he instead paid them wages for their work, which kind of compensation he was familiar with in his old world. Despite many sermons, he did not want the respect and honor that came with owning slaves and felt it was easier to handle the workers this way.

The workers responded in a complex way. Some people suppose that, when a man has his liberty, he proceeds to waste it by spending his wealth on anything but food and shelter, such as liquor and women. This was not so. Though the royalty of the city forbade commoners from spending on luxury goods, the workers saved their wages. They intended to use some of it for their children's education, some for a surety against old age, and dearer times when the city was in crisis or there were no more wars being fought.

Some supposed the workers would start businesses that rivaled and crushed our hero's. This was partially true. The workers did save their wages to start their own shops, and indeed eventually left our hero's employment to work full-time on their businesses. However, their businesses often complemented our hero's: for example, they started restaurants and wineries and used some products to start their own clothing stores. This enhanced our hero's business immensely. If the workers started their own gardens, he did not mind the competition at all, and felt it was justified.

The city's nobles and the king, seeing the city people so empowered, were frightened by this change, yet enjoyed wine and cheese so much they did not change any laws for the time being.

The businesswoman made a suggestion to our hero. He should purchase a large amount of land outside of the city, which could support nearly half of the city's workers. The land sat idle, as the owner had died a while ago and his children squandered its use, believing that they possessed too few slaves to make use of it. However, the city's laws only allowed royalty to purchase the land. Our hero should secure a sum large enough to buy the land, the king and his advisors' opinions, and possibly a title. If all went well, he could hire a man who had a skillful hand in growing flowers.

Thus our hero began his journey to become a businessman.

30

Our hero sought a loan from the princess. He believed he had good relations with her due to his adventure with the jackalope.

There was no jackalope to be found in her palace. In fact, there was not much of a palace anymore. The mansion had been sieged by the replacement's army to purge all of his predecessor's relations. This was a sound policy in the circumstances that any intended to take his crown from him.

Our hero found the princess's eunuch weeping over the ruins. He had been the princess's guardian since she was a young girl, and living without her drove him mad with grief. When our hero told him his predicament, he surmised that the replacement could not take all of the wealth away, as if it was very vast and diffuse. If the princess were present, she would invest in our hero's business in hopes of restoring her status.

Unfortunately a spy overheard this conversation and sent them to jail, as it was sound policy to disallow any citizen from mentioning the enemies of the state, in fear of fomenting dissent.

Upon entering the jail they learned, in those dark quarters where men had no hope of having anything that make life happy, men bartered in the currency of terror. Prisoners terrorized their companions by raping them; the more a man raped, the more he was feared, the more he was able to convince his fellows and the guards, and the more other prisoners sought to be raped by him for their protection. The princess, being a beautiful woman, received the worst raping anyone had ever seen, but she reacted to it with indifference, and disappointment, and contempt, for their rapes were light compared to her parties. No matter whether they raped her in the shower or in the mess hall, she did not bat an eyelash. She used the spikes of the iron maiden as toys and played with herself in the bronze bull. She was unrapeable. This was how she rose to the heights of the jail's hierarchy.

She organized a jousting tournament for her own amusement. Each round had two men. Both would place a sheath resembling a horse over their member, and hold their erect member at round start. Given a signal, one man would receive the other's manhood in a shouting rush. Whoever cried uncle first lost. The eunuch was given a pickle.

Our hero won, not by virtue of his member, which was somewhat small, but by the reason that his rear was never bothered by the members of others. It had grown quite wide and the fat cushioned it. When the princess asked what his prize should be, he answered "Freedom". The other prisoners wanted freedom as well, and executed the guards, decorating the jail with their organs.

Thereafter they were freed, the princess replied she would only share her wealth with a husband, examined our hero's genitals, and found them of insufficient size.

31

The princess told our hero and the eunuch what she desired from a husband. They searched throughout the land, for a suitor.

They poured plaster into the princess's genitals, creating a cast of it. They then sought the tallest, most handsome, brawniest, and wealthiest princes, with tattoos, around and asked them to take a stab at it. None of the princes were able to fit into it perfectly. They then asked the princes had any servants or slaves who could fit. Men and women alike could not satisfy the cast. They then asked if any of their fists could fit into the cast. This could not be fulfilled either.

Downcast and tired, our heroes sought rest at a castle built over a swamp, as questionable the hospitality of a castle over a swamp is. Nevertheless the host was very gracious and treated our heroes lavishly, for the host was the manpig who was still infatuated with our hero.

The manpig tried to woo our hero with the brightest of jewels, the most colorful of flowers, the most sumptuous of feasts, the best of songs and theaters, and the greatest of flatteries. Our hero declined each of these romantic overtures.

The manpig then offered to invest in our hero's business. Our hero gave his assent to go to his bedroom.

On hearing this happy news, the manpig's member swelled, filled with lust. It nearly tossed his robes over his head. For the manpig had employed a magician to increase its size thrice, as well as his confidence, in an effort to find a partner, though he found it odd less than zero partners were attracted to his new self. The eunuch gasped and tried the cast on him. It fit. The eunuch was elated, our hero was not. Our hero's heart sunk.

The manpig gave our hero the strongest of aphrodisiacs, ordered him to shower, and then, in the most voluptuous robes, to follow a trail of rose petals to his bedchamber. Our hero did so, and found the manpig hidden under the covers of a canopy bed, where he was the fifth pillar.

Our hero, though he thoughtlessly agreed, could not do this. He hit and kicked the member, whose tip was bigger than his head, which stimulated it even more. It was unfortunate the maids shackled his hands together in the bath, and the manpig easily wrestled our hero down, finally removing the covers from his eager member. It resembled a tree trunk with its veins as thick as snakes, and the mere sight of it caused out hero to faint, that and the sedatives the manpig put into his wine.

The manpig placed the tip, as large as a soldier's helmet, into our hero, and felt joy that he could push more and more of the helmet into our hero, and larger and larger the manpig's heart grew on feeling acceptance in the throes of his body. He had for so long been rejected by the world as a result of what the witch had turned him into he felt only despair for his future. More and more it entered our hero until the manpig entered his final gruntings; he quickly retreated it, and released his delight into the air like spring rain, spraying our hero's back, shooting at the canopy, so that it fell, and staining the bed and the carpet in his joy. He turned our hero's face around, which was good luck, as he might have drowned, and gave him a kiss goodnight, before he too slept.

Our hero, when he awoke, asked the eunuch to help him flee at midnight, for he could not walk; everything from his stomach to his legs ached in intense pain. They fled with moonlight on their backs, the hero with white on his, and reported what they knew to the princess. The princess then added a new specification to the resumé.

Our hero and the eunuch returned to the manpig and found the mask the princess gave them fit on his head. They then offered the princess's hand in marriage. The manpig agreed on the condition our hero became his mistress. Our hero agreed also with the contract, and plotted to get out of it, for he wanted to live.

32

The business of our hero received a request. In a castle situated on a crag overlooking a deep abyss, a necromancer ruled alone an army of undead. He despaired of his own immortality and wanted to feel the pleasure of life again, and so sought the vessel of an adult male.

Our hero inquired after the sisters. The sisters were doing well. As they shared some blood with men, they did not suffer much deterioration from the death of the forest god. Their hair had fallen out, their skin wrinkled, and their muscles atrophied, but they were still able to farm and hunt, for the other creatures suffered far more than they. They also did not put too much stock in beauty. Hair was the primary means by which their species attracted mates, but it was not unheard of in the animal world for females to choose their males rather than the other way around.

The sisters guided our hero to a slime grove and taught him the means to catch one, using jars. They then taught him how to feed and domesticate the slime. He thanked them and went on his way.

Our hero responded to the necromancer's request by mating with the slime, thereby producing an offspring. This the necromancer could use as a vessel. The hero requested specific payment. He would produce another child, but he wished the necromancer, using his dark magic, to accelerate this one's aging so he could provide it to the manpig. The necromancer agreed.

The necromancer aged the child and, through a ritual,

separated his soul from his body and entered the now adult replica of our hero. The necromancer then disemboweled himself and became spirit again. The vessel was too stupid for him.

Our hero asked the recruiter to find a pregnant woman of suitable reputation. When the necromancer agreed with the choice, they placed the woman in a magic circle, and the necromancer's spirit entered the unborn child. The woman went into labor immediately; the head broke out; then the arms; then the necromancer crawled out on his own strength, in adult form, for he did not want to wait through adolescence. The woman, understandably, died.

He then disemboweled himself with a knife meant for the umbilical cord. The horrors of being born convinced him to hate life and wish for the lack of sensation again.

His soul flew around the room, until it entered the only suitably blank vessel, the womb of the woman's pet bird, who then laid the egg. Our hero sought to sell this egg, for he thought it would have a discerning taste.

Without the necromancer's command, the undead army roamed mindlessly. Our hero retrieved the former necromancer's records and exhorted the mage to learn them.

33

The mage had explained to our hero that, through a catalyst, a wizard can manipulate the four major elements, fire, water, earth and wind, by molding them into something useful. The healer had heard this and did not correct the mage. There were many more elements than these four, and the fundamentals of magic involved using the catalyst, whose form represented the complexity of the universe, as a metaphor for the current one wanted to manipulate. He did not correct her as this was dangerous knowledge.

She was confused by the necromancer's depiction of a soul, which was made of no substance she recognized. Because she was ignorant, she thought this was impossible, though it had clearly been done, and told our hero so, as she had quashed our hero's dream of becoming a mage as he could not relate to any element. Our hero replied that he did not really need her services for his business any longer. So she resumed her studies.

She consulted her mentor, who oversaw her thesis paper. This same mentor had been glad to be rid of her, seeing that she had no potential but much gold, and only paid her the visit on the promise of more gold. Tantalized by the necromancer's extensive research, he retreated from his stance that necromancy was a forbidden art, pursued the notes passionately, and incidentally taught his former pupil how to bind his soul into an artifact. Thus this wise man, who denied himself the pleasures of the body for a life of study, became encapsulated in an amulet.

This same necklace was worn by the mage's husband, who was now endowed with the mentor's knowledge. More intelligent than he had been before, he understood the notes, aged our hero's replica, finished several of the necromancer's own experiments, and began divorce proceedings from his wife, for his newfound knowledge caused him to realize marriage was a chain. He failed to mentioned he had been seeing other, richer women.

Our hero did not think it was in his position to interfere, until he learned the minotaur sought to patent the necromancer's spells, which he had failed to do in his lifetime, and therefore raise astronomically the price of the spell's usage. He then thought it best to have the relationship mended. This would be difficult as the minotaur guarded the amulet ardently.

The minotaur was courting a wealthier, smarter woman and had taken her for a carriage ride into the countryside. Our hero arranged for one of the wheels to fall out during the ride. He had hoped the subsequent fall would cause his head to be hit, lowering his intelligence. Instead, his body was impaled on a tree branch, severing any use of his lower body.

With this infirmity, our hero and the mage easily took the amulet away. To cure her husband's disability, the mage learned a spell, which grafted her husband's upper body with a cow's lower body. Her husband then produced fresh, delicious milk for her every day, which compensated partially the temporary grief he caused her. She kept the other lower half for her own amusement.

34

In her grief over her divorce the mage poured her heart and soul into learning the necromancer's spells, and became quite good at casting them. In normal life, the image of the soul is aligned with the image of the body; necromancy severs and creates differences between the two images. On some days she imagined the soul as a fish, on other days she imagined it as water, and her task consisted of guiding the soul to its proper place.

She became so successful at these spells noblewomen supplied her with other women whose features they desired. She began a successful business in grafting.

The replica was delivered, and an extravagant wedding was planned. The replacement, though he ordered for the princess's imprisonment, would attend, for free wine was offered, and kings much love having things without paying their price.

The preparations had a flaw, however. The replacement loved roast pig. Our hero's company was sought after. Fortunately a roasted pig of appropriate size was found when the manpig had a heart attack. The doctor stiffly surmised there was one large reason as to why he was not receiving proper blood circulation.

Now the wedding had no groom.

Our hero found the pigman, who was a forest creature conceived when the forest god in the form of a pig conceived with a human woman. He convinced him to replace the manpig. To cover his alopecia, the mage grafted his predecessor's hair onto him. His limp had to be supported by a cane. Then the mage made the most important touch. However, this touch, due to rigor mortis, was constantly erect. The member was given a hat and clothes and supposed to be the manpig's mistress.

As brides do, the princess got cold feet and ordered our hero to cancel the wedding. She was an honorable person and did not retract her promise of treasure, after much convincing by the eunuch.

The wedding was well-beloved. The replacement drank much, ate much pork, and did not notice the manpig, who was a close friend unfortunately transmogrified by a witch, was barely comprehensible, for he too was unable to hold a conversation, never needing the skill.

The priest read the bride and groom their vows, prefacing that each of them could be refunded with gold. The pigman collapsed, fed much poison. The attendants of the wedding plunged their swords into the mistress, assuming she was the assassin, and had blood and other fluids cover them.

The princess wept, canceled the remainder of the event, and sent roasted pieces of the groom as consolation. She ordered our hero to save the phallus. As it had lost much blood, the mage grafted it onto the eunuch and redirected the blood away from him and towards the man, in the same vein a tree draws water and nutrients from its soil. The phallus rejuvenated, and, where the eunuch perished, his consciousness was transferred to the phallus. The arrangement was satisfactory for all parties, for the eunuch only existed to please his ward, and the princess did not like that the eunuch talked so much. In fact, the princess liked this so much that she relayed to the replacement that the witch had returned again, turned his friend into a phallus, and she sought to marry the phallus. This also pleased the replacement who also did not like to talk, and her subsequent marriage restored her reputation in the eyes of the royalty.

As for the replica, who sighed in relief when the manpig deceased, his freedom was bought by the princess, as she liked to watch.

35

Before our hero could acquire the princess's treasure, he had to attend to the mage's needs.

She began relying on undead creatures for comfort. She had a pair of undead dogs, an undead maid to attend to her pets, and sought to reanimate her husband so she could have an undead son and daughter, after which she would take from herself the sensation of living. Beside risking their business relationship, the prosecutor relayed to our hero that undead pets were not allowed in the city.

The mountains nearby had volcanic vents that made for excellent saunas. Our hero and his valuable business partner, after many adventures, sojourned there.

The water scalded her skin, the masseuse was too rough, she broke a nail and she was on the rag. She was unable to get a good night's sleep as she dreamt always the day her husband aspired for divorce. It did not help women paid great attention to her husband, if only because cow milk was a scarcity in the mountains.

A favorite recreation introduced to the saunas involved smothering the patrons in dung. Evidently this was a taste acquired in the former king's palace. The smell from this pastime further did not improve the mage's mood.

She hated life even more bitterly and only wished to return home to create unliving abominations.

The princess and her husband spent their honeymoon here, along with a large entourage of men. Their day-to-day activities consisted of sweating and foreign liquids, in the saunas and out of them. Though they invited our heroes, this did not improve the mage's mood.

When our hero woke up the next morning, he found the mage had slain and reanimated the proprietor's children and pretended they were her own. Unfortunately, their rotting flesh boiled in the saunas. Fortunately, the proprietress assumed they were boiling meat, and, as beef was also a scarcity in the mountains, made beef stew for the guests that day.

The princess's husband, otherwise known as the phallus, formerly known as the eunuch, enjoyed approaching women other than his wife, cornering them, and spitting on them voluminously, covering their bodies. He enjoyed this with zeal, as he had little to no opportunity to do so in his prior life. The eggs in his spittle were the size of salamanders, slid up the woman's womb, and came out as phallus children. This was becoming a bit much for everyone other than the princess, and our heroes intervened.

Our hero restrained the phallus by his phimosis, took a knife, entered his arm with the knife into the tip of the phallus, and with the mage's knowledge of anatomy severed the vans deferens. This did not stop the phallus's aggressive behavior, but this did prevent unwanted children.

From this ordeal the mage learned the value of life, and learned never to use her awesome powers to alter life, unless the requisite gold was given.

When the proprietors learned what was in the beef soup, they sought vengeance on our heroes. The businesswoman, unable to convince them to take compensation, partnered with the prosecutor to sue them on the grounds of libel and distress, punished them by removing their freedom, bought them, and sent them far away on cruel tasks so they would not bother our hero's business any longer. This allowed the businesswoman to buy the spa as well; the partnership with our hero's business allowed for better services, which pleased the customers.

36

The princess possessed vast veins of gold, but had neither the wisdom nor patience to use it. She sold shares in the mine and bought shares back when convenient for her, on nothing but the wealth that could be generated by a mine and on the strength of her reputation. Without credit, our hero would have to seize the land itself. However, due to the scarcity of the lands surrounding the city, the diseased forest creatures prowled the wastes for even the smallest bite.

The businesswoman had a simple but effective plan. She appealed to their pride as rulers of this land not too long ago, permitting the humans to live on their own leisure, and convinced them to take fortune into their own hands and work hard for their offspring. They were allotted forty acres of land; they did not need the mule as some of them were. They entered into a partnership with our hero's business, exchanging some crops for gold, which in turn could be exchanged for meat and other luxuries.

However, they lacked the knowledge to grow food, so they were given education for a fee. Regardless of their strength and speed, they still required tools, which were lent for a fee. Some could not use tools without hands, and so were punished with a fine. As the land they were given was arid, they could grow very little, and thus did not meet certain quotas, which were necessary for our hero's business to draw some profit, and they had to pay a fine. Finally, they were unable to provide enough for themselves and their families, which inability, because it violated welfare laws, forced them to pay a fine. The carnivores died, the herbivores starved, until only the coprophages lived, only barely. Many died by drinking their sorrows away. The somewhat tilled, somewhat cultivated land was then given over to humans, which was fortunate for our hero's business.

Our heroes made their way to the gold veins. They were taken aback when they found, instead of vast stores of gold-banded rock, a golden palace, with a golden roof, a golden door, and golden windows, which were very hard to see through. A golden butler led them inside, and golden maids catered to their needs. A golden king explained that the patriarch's death had weakened the magical boundaries of the realm, allowing golden elementals, beings whose nature were not carbon but of gold, to dwell in the gold veins and create a palace of it. Then they bred and created more golden people and pets. They showed them how they bred; it was very loud.

Though our hero and the businesswoman were pleased there was even more gold than imagined, and in a cultivated state, they were displeased that it had feelings. That night, a golden lantern cracked in the golden palace, causing a golden fire, which, by being of gold, set the golden palace ablaze. Contrary to how one would think, golden water did not douse golden flame, and the golden elementals, for the same hazards they felt the need to escape their golden realm, were burned to liquid gold.

Our heroes rejoiced. The princess would be very pleased with the increase in her wealth, and the forest creatures could be given free gold so as to escape the cycle of poverty and therefore death. The businesswoman thought differently.

The influx of gold into the city, so vast it was, immediately diluted the value of gold, which markedly decreased the value of nearly all of their possessions. In short, the rich were poor, and, as our hero had to pay his workers more gold as a result of the actual value of the gold, the poor were not rich but less poor. The forest creatures could do nothing with this devalued gold but, as the businesswoman lowered the price of alcohol, drank even more quickly to death. The replacement contemplated basing the city's currency on corn, but found it was difficult to boast about his wealth in corn. The princess was far less wealthy than she had been before, and our hero, not understanding that wealth is generated by the value of labor, which value comes from the ability to purchase the necessaries of life such as staple foods, was not that much wealthier and no closer to acquiring land.

37

Our hero, during his adventure to find a suitor for the princess, who for all intents and purposes was now a pauper, found one other investor. He concluded this investor could only be a last resort. The dwarves provided him with incredible armor. He wrote a will providing for his child dragon and donned the armor as he made his way into the dark castle.

The castle's exterior was adorned with sculptures of devils impaling humans. Its air was foul and yet cold. The fountain of the plaza flowed with blood.

When our hero entered, he was greeted by three succubi. These ladies were very beautiful, so he agreed to remove his armor.

The host would not attend dinner, so our hero had to be comforted by these ladies. They ate human eyes as an hors d'oeuvre, roasted human women, pregnant with child, as the main course, and chilled human brains cooked in rosemary for dessert. Our hero did not know they were human and so ate happily, as his hostesses frequently related how hot the room was and removed more and more articles of clothing.

Our hero was then taken to a guest room, where his hostesses placed themselves on the same couch in very compromising positions. Our hero, having never been with a woman, except a very lucky doe, was not compelled to make love with them. This was fortunate, as their vaginas were lined with razor sharp teeth.

Finally, the host led him into his office. The office was dark, and his head was aflame.

This was one of the four demon lords, upon whom the fate of the world hinged upon.

Our hero presented his business's strengths and the fruits to be had for an investor. The demon lord listened little. In his eyes he owned everything in the world. He simply thought of ways to have fun.

The demon lord approved the loan. Our hero bribed the replacement and his advisors and purchased the large tract of land. He hired a great deal of men to work on the farm; some were skilled, most were hardworking, and those who were not talented in this type of work were treated charitably by our hero, such that skilled and hardworking people were drawn to the farm. The farm was doing well in several ways: it brought our hero and his friends a great deal of gold; it provided quality goods that other cities sought; and it increased the wealth of its workers, who themselves would purchase their own farms. The workers, whose sole security prior to this was to sell their bodies and souls to the nobles for the possibility, not the surety, of a scrap of bread, were content as they were finally captains of their own lives. This contentment would lead to only one conclusion.

Our hero was arrested and brought before court. The prosecutor accused him of fomenting dissent and plotting to assassinate the replacement, who is the king. Her evidence consisted of our hero evading his own assassination.

For example, our hero refused to eat a poisoned pie. He simply thought the boy should have had it.

He dodged the garotte in his own bed. He had wondered why the circulation in his right arm was so bad.

He sidestepped a crossbow bolt. He thought someone had installed a peg for his keys.

As he clearly knew of his own assassination, he knew his life was in mortal danger, and thus he knew he was revenged by the king's friends and allies. He therefore attempted to assassinate the king. This was the worst crime, and so he had to be executed.

This verdict upset the peasantry greatly, who responded by setting the courthouse on fire. They would have stormed the replacement's new palace had his royal guard not assembled around it. They promised to return with more armaments.

Fortunately for our hero, he was replaced by his clone, the phallus's plaything. The prosecutor, to save her own neck, gave our hero a lenient sentencing and put him in jail indefinitely. The prisoners were not allowed to rape him, so he ingratiated himself to them, using his greatly-widened rear, by blowing wind on them in the poorly-circulated prison during very hot days.

Our hero disliked the death and destruction and judged, rightly, that the farm could not succeed during a war, and he could not grow flowers for the goddess. The businesswoman agreed. However, the business for making weapons would prosper.

38

The war proceeded in twists and turns. The replacement asked for the best of arms and armor to be forged for him, as he felt the stirrings of war in his blood from his career as a general. Unfortunately, since then, he had added quite a bit of weight. He was equipped with armor, he walked down the stairs to a crowd of admiring onlookers, and he fell down those stairs, and died.

The rebels' cheer was short-lived. They could not agree on a campaign. Some wanted to execute the monarchists by hanging. Others wanted to execute them by ax. Some wanted to slay them and impale their heads on pikes, and some wanted to immolate them. As they could not agree, they warred with one another, formed conspiracies, and did to their comrades what they would to their foes.

In desperation the rebels petitioned the city in the desert to raise an army for them. They pleaded to their old enemies their cause for freedom and prosperity. The folk of the desert recalled how often they themselves paid for that same freedom and prosperity. They concluded this was a just cause, so long as they were able to plunder. At the first assault, the city's defenses crumbled, and the soldiers raped and looted to their heart's content. When the rebels could not pay them more, they promptly left and related to their families the astounding raping and looting they had accomplished. The monarchists and the rebels fought over ruins, but they were ruins dearly beloved.

Seeing this, the businesswoman thought it unwise to lend

the services of the dwarves to either the rebels or the monarchists. Instead, she set them to working on an explosive that could be propelled through the air and into an enemy camp, ending the war effectively for one side or the other. The dwarves were ingenious smiths and constructed an ingenious bladder, but knew not what to put into it.

Our hero searched far and wide for deadly substances. He conceived of poisons, but no scorpion was willing to part with it. He conceived of fire elementals, but he was not willing to pay health insurance. He conceived of disease, but no corpse would have intercourse with him.

Our hero considered what he himself most associated with death, and thereby discovered what to put into the explosive.

He and the dwarves went to retrieve the gas from the former king's palace, the king preceding the replacement. The businesswoman approved, and demonstrated its use on cattle. High in the air the bladder went; then it fell; and upon striking the ground erupted in a vast explosion of stench, where grass wilted. The goblins, whose village our heroes used as a testing ground, were found not to have died from shock, but from the wounds caused by tearing their noses off their faces.

Both sides were awed, saw the merit of this type of poison, and did not purchase it. Instead, they sought to create it on their own. They gathered all of their soldiers and chattel, had them eat as much cheese and lentils as they required, and relieved themselves into a trench. They then filled their own bladders with smell. On the very same day, at the very same time, both bladders went up into the air, blotting the sun, fell, and exploded; but they produced no effect, as both sides, in

the past days, acclimated to their own flatulence. The war
went on.

39

Our heroes were in the process of crafting a new weapon when a detachment of the monarchists attacked. Led by the prosecutor, they overwhelmed our heroes, who had no martial skills, for the soldier, who was very brave, sought to fight and die for both sides, as it was not in a soldier's mind to question his allegiance.

The prosecutor informed them that the replacement of the replacement was by no means a wise king, and it was to the monarchists' advantage as well as our heroes that he were deposed. If our heroes aided in her conspiracy, she would grant them amnesty and freedom as they wished. To this, our heroes complied.

Immediately our heroes lifted the embargo of goods to the monarchists. They purchased, on credit, food, drink and arms aplenty, and thus gained the upper hand in the war, as the rebels were still fractured and friendless among neighbors. The monarchists praised the replacement's replacement, as the replacement's replacement was the type to take praise well.

During one celebratory feast, when the replacement's replacement bit into the leg of a roasted duck, he became deathly white, and foamed at the mouth. As quickly as they could our heroes sent him an antivenom. Promptly he revived, and led his troops into the heart of the rebels' camps, crushing them.

Having now routed the rebels, he was in the process of bargaining for peace among the remnants. Peace, to him and his forebears, was to surrender their necks to nooses and their women into captivity. The rebels disliked this concession and mounted a desperate assault on the monarchists' camp. Our heroes discovered this through a spy, disguised in the tailor's clothing, and hired a guild of carpenters to fortify the monarchists' defenses. The assault was frustrated, and the rebels had to part with their necks.

The replacement's replacement was overjoyed and ordered a triumph, which our heroes obliged. The dwarves fashioned chariots in brilliant gold, the recruiter found litter-bearers, and the businesswoman procured barrels of wine. The triumph occurred on a sunny day, where the men were handsome, the women beautiful, and everyone smiled, until the prosecutor drove her dagger into the replacement's replacement's heart. His army did not mind, as he contemplated burying them alive as his army eternal. Unfortunately, the rebels thereupon regrouped and regained territory, and then some.

Our heroes felt they had accomplished their goal of destroying the monarchists and were content with it, until the prosecutor, who was now the queen, summoned them to court. She accused them of treason and sought to have them executed.

Our heroes equipped the amulet of wisdom on the mage's husband, the half-minotaur, half-cow. Immediately he wrote an impassioned defense on behalf of our heroes' rights, claiming that they could not deny their sovereign's requests. It was unfortunate that this argument did not fly under the new regime, whose sovereign was not the replacement's replacement but the prosecutor.

The mage's husband argued that they had attempted to kill

the king, but were very incompetent. Considering they had been the cause of everyone else but the king's deaths, this argument did not fly.

Our heroes gathered together on the final days of the trial, and submitted their final argument. The replacement's replacement and the prosecutor's arguments were illegitimate, thus their laws could not be obeyed. Neither had an ounce of dragon's blood. Further, our hero had this divine blood. As the queen was to announce that blood was not a determining factor for royalty as a result of martial law, a noble drove his dagger into her heart.

Nevertheless our hero was not king for long, lest he lose his heart too. The monarchists established a parliament in absence of a king, and the mage's husband demanded a divorce.

40

The mage took her second divorce much more easily. She was however not pleased to part with half of her possessions. Our heroes argued to her husband that, without a stable government, no one could certify their divorce. He relented.

Our heroes traveled to the city over the sands, though they were reluctant to. They were regarded as a dirty, bloody race, whose passions were only for fighting and copulating. They did not use toilets, they did not wipe after defecating, they did not clean their sidewalks, they did not say "Please" and "Excuse me", they did not ask a woman's permission to hold their hand. They believed only in violence, which certainly was the opposite of the beliefs of the city of the forest. Also their skin was very dark.

Nevertheless, our heroes petitioned their king to intervene in the conflict and to aid the rebels. The king, who was an unreasonable man and believed in fake gods, and who was very hairy, reasoned that the cause of war came from the king's lineage, and that if royal rule were abolished and the commons set up government, the city of the forest would either weaken significantly, allowing the folk of the desert to flourish, or they would desire peace, as the many prefer peace over the few. Because he was very stupid and a heathen, and his mind was poisoned by his people's nonsensical language and their badly-written texts written by very dark hands, he consulted his advisors, who were also deficient in understanding but less so than him. He agreed with our heroes and delivered regiments to the rebels; these regiments were paid so that they would do neither looting nor ravaging. The rebels only accepted them after consulting their blessed, very wise, and very real animal gods who were dead.

The monarchists were promptly defeated by the ungodly, savage, heathen, yet very orderly and very disciplined army of the desert. The rebels set up government, and their first order was to throw their gaseous bombs onto the city of the desert, as it was very wise to destroy one's enemies a long time before they were to declare war. The citizens, unaccustomed to the rebels' flatulence, deceased in droves, and the rebels' gods rewarded them with much looting and ravaging that day. In fact, the looting and raping had been so good that the rebels and the monarchists bonded, and they were equal in spirit as they were under the law.

The rebels adopted the monarchists' parliamentary government. The rebels thought this was a good idea, the monarchists thought this was a good idea, and the monarchists' slaves thought this was a good idea as the monarchists fed them, even though they were considered half a person under the new laws.

The government now stabilized, our heroes argued that the lower half of the mage's husband belonged to the mage. The government honored the divorce and bisected the husband in half. As her husband was now deceased, there was no need to transfer half of the mage's possessions over.

41

As for the clone, as he would not be executed under the new government, he instead was used as a sword-holder, and was well-beloved by the soldiers. A mysterious person donated to his electoral campaign, and he was accepted into parliament easily.

In his first speech, the clone, who was formerly the eunuch's asshole, flattered the citizens greatly, calling them brave, calling them strong, and saying they were blessed by their gods, who were dead. In the asshole's second speech, he praised them on behalf of their heritage and their history for overcoming adversity. In his third speech, he lambasted those citizens who did not participate in the wars, and asked that they be executed for treason. In his fourth speech, he questioned the allegiances of certain, impure citizens. In his fifth speech, he demanded camps be built. Our hero and the dwarves were placed into camps for their rehabilitation. Their fellow citizens tried to gas them, but our heroes had smelled worse odors. The dwarves were used to the smell of deceased bodies for centuries. They could only be locked up and starved.

This was our hero's chance for losing weight and getting abs, yet he felt unfulfilled in this situation.

Many creatures of the forest were arrested too. The doe had been captured. She entreated our hero to touch her stomach. He felt a kick, and immediately understood. He petitioned the doe to be gassed first, but, alas, the paperwork was not processed quickly enough and a half-calf half-boy was born. The clone hailed this as a triumph of humanity and exalted the doe and the boy as icons to the supremacy of their blood. They were not to be executed. However, being deer, they still had to live in the camp.

As the state unfortunately could not give each of the detainees what they desired i.e. death immediately, they set them on certain useless tasks until they could be processed. Our hero and the dwarves made weapons that no soldier used, they made goods that no one consumed, and they made many lamps out of the corpses of their fellow inmates. These had great potential value among the citizens, but as our hero's business could not in some way redistribute these goods in an efficient way they instead laid in an enormous stockpile, kept under guard by a watchman, who because of the superiority of his blood felt he could sleep most hours of the job and work the last hour by eating his sandwich.

The doe asked our hero to wipe the calf, the doe asked our hero to rock the calf to sleep, the doe asked our hero to watch the calf as she joined her friends in her book club. This proved too much for our hero.

Our hero, receiving his weekly allotment of venison, noticed the tatters of a baby's clothing tangled in his fork. He said nothing, removed the shreds, and continued eating. When the doe inquired after their child, he felt inadequate at answering the question.

The boy was eventually found. He had removed his clothing, cantered to the butchery, remarked how sharp the knives were, cantered to the ovens, remarked how hot the fires were, cantered out, and tripped on a fallen blade. The animals made relics of the boy's lower half and the citizens made relics of the boy's upper half, and so, with their respective martyrs, the two species went to war.

Our hero took advantage of the pell-mell. The dwarves crafted pickaxes, and they dug their way out of the camp. Soon thereafter, the animals broke from the camps and released themselves, and the doe demanded a divorce. They were to finalize their divorce by the pope of the forest.

42

Though the forest and the city in the past shared very few communications, the city, upon seeing their citizens take the historic lands of the forest creatures, cultivate them, and banish them from their ancestral homes through bloodshed, such that their only recourse was to take up the bottle and complain, felt something like compassion for the forest folk and allowed them to govern their own people under their own laws though they inhabited what was now predominantly the city's lands. Eager to use their newfound rights, the forest creatures created laws, for historically they had none, except for those that promoted the survival of the strongest. Our hero could not resist his divorce and had to be subjected to the authority of the pope of the forest.

The pope of the forest was an ancient dragon, who in his younger days devoted his heart and soul to the god of the forest, and whose faith was rewarded by the same god, who was dead. When that god was still alive, he argued that the god rewarded compassion and decency shown to their fellow animals. This was harder to argue now that this same god was deceased, and compassion was measured by mouthfuls of food.

The pope ignored our hero's divorce and brought up an entirely new charge: that of miscegenation. Only the former god of the forest could mix blood between man and animal. This was punishable by death.

Our hero sought counsel. The mage summoned the spirits of her husband and the prosecutor, attaching her husband's upper half with the attorney's bottom half, creating a female minotaur with two lifetimes of experience in law. This minotaur also had breasts. Unfortunately, the minotaur was a quarter animal, and thus was afforded with a quarter of the rights given to animals. Upon realizing this, she transplanted herself to the forest folk's side and became a prosecutor.

Our heroes sought out one of the pope's bishops for counsel, slew him, and replaced his head with the phallus, formerly the princess's eunuch. The pope did not notice his bishop's transformation as in his prior life he was also a dickhead. Unfortunately, the phallus was as unintelligible as the former bishop, and was thus ignored. He had to be content sodomizing little boys.

Finally, our heroes consulted the sisters. The sisters had a superior grasp of the laws of the forest than our heroes did, as a result of being favorites of the former god, and sought to settle the matter in a duel, as there were no laws in the forest. The mighty dragons assented. The duel would be waged in basketball.

Though dragons are renowned for their aerial abilities, their posture and manual dexterity did not allow for good dribbling. They stumbled through the first, second, third and fourth quarters. The pope heckled his team, threatened to excommunicate his bishops, and raised all sorts of blackmail, yet nevertheless they lost. He would have to be satisfied with their crucifixion for their lack of zeal for their god, who was dead.

As final rites, the pope demanded our hero kiss his feet a thousand times. He then demanded our hero flog himself a thousand times, and pray not to be a human in the next life.

He then demanded our hero eat the waste of a thousand animals. When this was no longer funny he released him.

It was then the dragon's egg hatched.

The pope rejoiced, for it was a baby without blemish. As a token of intimacy, he and the baby touched nostrils. He recoiled, for it was the child of himself and his niece. He ordered the baby to be executed. The bishops, who were in the process of being crucified, had had enough, and revealed all of the pope's sexual indiscretions, with this and that boy, covered in roses and whip cream, with wooden paddles, et cetera. The animals beat the pope, tore his wings off, and gelded him, and for every boy he sodomized he was sodomized in turn, which justice was difficult to enact, for he enjoyed centuries of sodomy.

Our hero and the doe, though they had discovered the other was not a good person, agreed to remarry to take care of the baby dragon.

43

As the dickhead enjoyed sodomy, he sought to alleviate his pope's burdens. He was seen as a saint for this act of charity, and thus through this influence was able to build a new church. With the businesswoman's assistance, he gave sermons concerning a god who rewarded their struggles in wealth with wealth, on the condition they gave him his wealth. In exchange, he would give them his seed, usually enough to fill their hands or mouths, which would eventually bless them with fortune. The animals, having very little wealth, liked this message, and spread wide and far the dickhead's words. Thus the dickhead became very popular.

The first act of his church was to wage a holy war against the city, who had recently awarded the asshole with a lifetime appointment as prime minister.

The businesswoman had learned her lesson and did not direct the business' energies into weapons-making. However, she did encourage the two heads of state to settle the matter peacefully. Though they hated the other by their blood, and by the fact that one had been sodomized by the other, they found they had much in common, in that they liked power, they liked orgies, and they liked sending innocent people to die. The two gave presents to the other, the one an entourage of boys to sodomize, the other an entourage of animals to shove up his ass.

Indeed, because the two adversaries liked the other so much, and resembled the other so much, they exerted themselves to make the war all the bloodier, as a kind of friendly rivalry. Every day innocent men died, every day innocent women were raped, and children orphaned, every day the dickhead sodomized and was sodomized, such that his palace from one wing to the other was occupied by an immense train of flesh, every day the asshole shoved more and more animals up his ass until he could hardly sit anymore.

As our hero and the doe belonged to neither camp, they sat this one out. They lived with the sisters, who were happy to have guests. The sisters no longer fed our hero corn husks, our hero no longer slept with the pigs, and our hero did not want to make love to the sisters, thus his wife was not possessive of him, and so they got along peacefully and even happily as the war between species intensified.

The dickhead was so happy in his idyll of sodomizing children, convincing men and women to die and to give up all of their wealth before they died, such that they lived in profound enough misery and suffering that death looked a good fate, for the dickhead sermonized that a heaven with their loving father awaited them, that he forgot he was married.

The princess, having lost all of her wealth, as a result of not understanding the concept of market saturation, was pleased with her husband's newfound fortune and the increase in intensity of his sexual activities. However, it was difficult to have two members of the household with voracious sexual appetites, and she often found more human resources were expended on her husband than herself.

To appease her jealousy, the dickhead made love to his wife, a while after they last made love. He put his head deeper and deeper into her, pushed more and more deeply, until he found a place within her without any light, and consequently no air, and thus began choking. He convulsed inside her; she enjoyed the foreplay; her husband deceased inside of her genitals, and he had not found the g-spot quite yet.

The asshole had received another shipment of animals to shove up his ass. One of them was the werewolf, a patriot who loved his fellow animals. When the asshole made to use him, the werewolf bit his buttchecks, such that they grew hair and teeth themselves. The asshole was now half-wolf, half-ass, a kind of being he despised, and so flew out of the city on his paws.

The half-man half-wolf half-asshole encountered our hero, who was strolling with his wife and child. Our hero's blood, having once been half-wolf, sensed another werewolf's blood, and he became a werewolf once more. The asshole leapt; our hero leapt also; they bit their fangs into the other; the asshole reeked; the asshole bled; our hero triumphed; but wolves are natural predators of deer, and so he had to sleep in the doghouse from now on.

The princess could not remove her husband's head from her body, and so was now actually part dragon, fulfilling her father's wishes of realizing his noble birth. She thus united the two sides, city and forest, through her realized heritage. Our heroes were able to return to the city, and our hero resumed his business, which the businesswoman had so handily attended for him while he was away.

44

Our hero was now able to hire a botanist. The doe assumed our hero's zeal for a botanist came from a love of horticulture.

The princess's reign inspired true harmony between the city and the forest, such that there was a resurgence of interest in forest culture. Citizens taught themselves the forest's many languages, they adopted the forest folk's dress and paint, and accepted some of their ethics. As the humans had, at some point in time, derived from the forest creatures, they were also able to recover thousands of years of lost history and science, which the forest folk did not develop.

These records detailed an old sage who lived deep in the forest and was wise in the lives of plants. Our hero, though unsure of this sage's health after the forest god's death, sought them out in hopes of beginning some form of investigation. He asked the sisters to aid him in tracking this sage. He also sought the recruiter, who would be able to negotiate a reasonable compensation for this expert.

Our hero also took with him the fire sprite, who was once a god of fire. Though the sprite disliked his imprisonment in the healer's lantern, he found his freedom more detestable. He had been hired as a heath for an inn, but in temperate weather he was unneeded, in colder days he received little wood, and when visitors extended their hands to him covered in frost, he was not allowed to devour them. He had been hired as a stove, but patrons liked their meat rare. He had been hired as a furnace, but metal gave him indigestion.

Finally he had been hired as a candle for an author, but the author never had any ideas. The sprite was starved and dispossessed, and so joined our heroes, on the promise he would not set anyone on fire, despite the protests of the sisters whose forest had once been the fire's buffet.

The road to the sage was long and arduous, as the signs then had long decayed, or were swept by the sands of the waste.

They encountered a sphinx, who gestured to ask three riddles, so as to eat them; but her throat was too hoarse, and so they passed her by.

They encountered a siren, who sang them a sweet song to entice them to drown; but when they walked to her rock, she became flustered and confounded, and left.

They encountered a squonk, who made to cry, and so vanished behind his tears; but he had no water to cry, and our heroes walked right past him, which made him all the sadder.

Our heroes discovered a lush oasis growing in the wastes. Large ferns obscured their vision, thick brushes blocked their path, and cheerful animals, who unfortunately did not speak the language of the forest, frolicked. They were all astounded such a thing could exist after the death of the forest god, and the sage, a dryad who alone remained of her kind, discreetly explained how this was by leading them.

In the center of the oasis was a fawn of white fur resting, around which flowers were fragrant, around which water was flowing, around which trees grew high. This was the god of the forest reborn.

The sisters rejoiced, for the forest would return, and, as the prior god had been their father, they wished to make love to the fawn. When pressed, the sage refused to return with our hero, as she needed to tend to the fawn's needs.

Our hero looked at his recruiter; the recruiter looked at the fire; the fire looked at our hero. They all agreed to return to the city.

The sisters spread the news to the forest folk, who rejoiced. They would soon retake the lands, slay the humans, and rule the new forests with their culture again. The businesswoman rejoiced too and congratulated them with gifts: shirts for their backs, shoes for their feet, hats on their heads. That the clothing had ticks on them bothered the forest folk little, for some of their neighbors were ticks.

As the ticks feasted on their blood, and regurgitated human blood into their veins, the forest creatures felt their claws dull, their teeth blunt, their veins withered, their strength dissipated. The sisters became shorter, they became weaker, they disliked basketball, they liked cooking, and they bought frilly dresses to wear. The animals became human, they stood upright, they became nervous, and anxious for the future, they wanted savings and welfare, which the city folk provided in compensation for their employment, they stopped believing in the forest god, the oasis's water dried, the flowers wilted, the trees became rotten, and the god of the forest stopped breathing one day.

Because the god of the forest was dead, again, the fire sprite did not break his promise by eating him, and the dryad settled for employment by our hero, lived with the grandmother, and bought a plant every week from the farmer's market.

45

Though the dryad was of simple means, in a certain season she was consumed by heat and had to mate. Because the dryad was so headstrong, for this was no caprice, but biological need, and because he was her employer, our hero felt he could not refuse, though he had a partner and a child. He did not tell the doe, and did not meet eyes with the dragon that morning, out of guilt and went to the solemn deed.

When he met the dryad she was bare to the waist. She ordered him to sit on the chair; he complied; she sat on his lap; he closed his eyes; her thighs were very soft; he became very hard; she became very heavy; she became unbearably heavy; he opened his eyes; she had become a tree, he was underneath this tree, and could not move.

The mage investigated, the sisters looked into it, the businesswoman read about it, the doe scolded him. The dryad's roots wrapped around our hero firmly; it was impossible to get him out without killing her. Meanwhile the roots entered his papilla, entered his urethra, and drained nutrients and water from him, which he very much felt; unless he ate and drank in great quantities, the dryad would drain him to death. He thus was given heaps of food to eat, and gallons of water to drink, and he felt his jaw close to falling apart, so tired were they.

As our hero was immobile, he had many hours to think on his light novel. It was clear that, because his protagonist was the hero, he was strong, intelligent, and just. It was clear that, because he was strong, intelligent, and just, women were quite attracted to him. It was clear that, because women were quite attracted to him, there could only be one he would truly be in love with. And it was clear that, because there was only one woman he loved, that same woman had to act as if she did not actually love him. This led to many scenes where she lost her clothes.

He had his wife transcribe his ideas, she did so slowly using her mouth. She understood very little the meaning behind them. When he attempted to explain, she stood, remained puzzled, and only knew now that these ideas were childish. Nevertheless she was patient and bore this task patiently.

The tree grew and grew, at a rate much faster than expected. The mage suspected that, as our hero's blood was of divine origin, so the pregnant dragon had told them, it possessed the material to grow into a divine tree. Our hero was concerned it would crush him. They wondered whether the dryad was any longer in it, and when she would return from maternity leave. The businesswoman summoned the adventurers to hack the roots of the tree; the dwarves smithed them strong axes; they chopped and they chopped, they were careful not to take off a certain member off our hero, they resorted to shears when they arrived to the more sensitive parts. Before they ultimately extracted our hero, they exchanged him with the pope, as the children had been exhausted of sodomizing him.

Our hero was freed, and the tree drank from the pope's veins. The tree could no longer be contained by the roof of the building, it touched the clouds, its head could no longer be seen in one's sight. The pope became one with the tree, happy to participate in something so great and grand at the end of his life, only for the tree to become a popular spot for citizens to stick their gum on, and for dogs to relieve themselves on.

46

It was unclear if the dryad were dead or alive; our hero endeavored to climb the tree and find out. He took with him the mage, the businesswoman and the soldier. The prosecutor, the half-minotaur, half-attorney, accompanied them, so as to determine whether our hero committed murder.

Our heroes climbed the great tree, whose crown disappeared in the vaults of heaven. Its bark was tough and gnarled, one could get little footholds into it, and creatures were already drawn to this resilient totem of life.

A wyrm chewed on the roots, but he only wanted some gum.

Harpies harangued our heroes at the heights, but they only wanted some soap to clean.

A roc had made its nest here, yet it found the tree too tall for its liking and desired some assistance down.

Our heroes, tired from rough climbing, plunged their faces into the clouds, showering themselves in suspended droplets; peering above, they found a vast expanse of white, and, to their surprise, a palace for giants in the vaporous clouds. It was painted in garish colors, it was as tall as the tree, and it was ornamented with dazzling gold and silver.

A shadow fell on them, and they heard the "earth" tremble around them, more and more intensely. They hid beneath a leaf; a giantess thundered by them and cut the top of the tree, keeping it short. She carried the tree, which was but a mustard green to her, back to her home; unbeknownst to her, she carried our heroes in her shoes.

The giantess paused in the path, and took off her shoes, for she felt sand in them. Our heroes scurried beneath her toenails, fitting themselves in the black lumps of dirt and dead skin. The giantess no longer felt the sand, but now she felt something in her toenails. Unfortunately she did not have her nail clippers at hand.

The giantess opened the immense doors to her palace, which her husband was renting, took off her shoes, and set down the mustard green in the kitchen and wondered how to cook it. Our heroes scurried away, yet only to the hideout they could quickly enter, the cracks of the wall.

No sooner did they enter were they jostled and bumped around by a hundred families of roaches, who were the same size as them; they touched our heroes all over with their antennae and teeth, and would have eaten them if they themselves had been eaten by larger roaches. The roaches carried them to successively larger roaches, until they arrived at a roach that had eaten several generations, who was born yesterday afternoon, and yet even this roach was devoured by the true lord of the walls, a rat whose head was the size of one of our heroes. The rat bared its teeth, making to eat our heroes. Our heroes ran.

Our heroes ran into a crevice even the rat could not squeeze into. They found a hairpin the giantess had forgotten. The five of them held up the hairpin and drove it into the rat's eye, piercing deeply into the brain.

The rat did not entirely decease. The mage had an idea. With her knowledge of anatomy, she entered the rat's skull, reorganized the rat's neurons, and found the rat could be manipulated. It was decided that our hero would pilot the rat, while the others resided in the stomach.

As soon as they made their way to the exit, they saw a goose on the giants' mantel. Although everything is very tall in the land of the giants, this goose was a dwarf, no bigger than the giantess's thumb, yet, as our heroes discovered, it laid golden eggs, which the giantess collected, being equal to pennies, though taxed nonetheless. The businesswoman was adamant in taking this goose, and our heroes had to agree. They also sought to see if the dryad was in the mustard green.

The half-dead, half-alive, very unhappy rat scurried throughout the house. Unfortunately, the giants kept a very bored cat.

The cat chased our heroes to the barn. The cat pounced; the rat ducked beneath the cow's hooves; the cow kicked the cat, breaking some teeth.

The cat chased our heroes to the kitchen. The cat pounced; the knives were put in hazardous places; the cat lost some hairs, and his manhood.

The cat chased our heroes to the kitchen. The cat pounced; ethanol was placed precariously; the cat lost some of his ability to speak and to walk.

The rat ran outside, where the neighbor's cat, a beautiful female, was crossing. The cat smiled; she did not appreciate his broken face; she further did not appreciate his alopecia, nor his missing manhood; he tried to speak; she found him unintelligible; he chased after her; she turned her tail to him. There was nothing for him to do but to hang his head with rope.

The cat was dispatched, and the giantess and her daughter sorely missed their pet. The giant, returning from a long day of drinking, scooped up the rat and put it in a cage in their infant daughter's room.

47

It was needless to say that our heroes were barely taller than the baby's foot, and thus she exerted much power over them. When she pounded on her wooden blocks, the earth shook. When she banged on the bars of her crib, their ears hurt.

The baby stripped our heroes of their clothing, as is one of the first curiosities a child has with their toys. As she was unfamiliar with male anatomy, she poked and prodded at our hero. She thought his anus was peculiar, and inserted her finger in there; our hero felt his insides might have burst, had she not tired of this exercise and put him in a milkmaid's dress.

The baby slapped our heroes around in a fictional bucolic town, threw them into buildings, and ran them over with trains, which the giantess noted to her husband were not part of the countryside, and were fortunately made of very light plastic.

The baby grabbed the soldier, dressed in a shepherd's outfit, put her gums over his head, and kept him in there, choking him. She then, in her children's curiosity, took her mother's scissors, and, satisfying another of a child's curiosities, cut his head off, his blood released in spurts, which delighted her. She spilled blood all over the carpet, then returned the headless soldier to his crook by his sheep, and then fell asleep on the blood, in which state she urinated an ocean into her diaper, and defecated a mountain, which mountains of many mushed peas our heroes unfortunately had to waft.

Our heroes acted quickly. They fled from their posts, and then cut pieces of the baby's diaper, dipping them into the bottle of whiskey the giant left behind, and poured whiskey into the bottle of milk. They then, with much disagreement among them, held onto a sewing needle left behind.

The baby awoke and, feeling hunger, groped for her milk. She became very drunk and stumbled through her wooden blocks and kicked aside her toy sheep, and found she barely had the mental faculties to manipulate any of our heroes. She cried; the giantess visited her, but found nothing wrong. She stumbled across her toys again, found she was still too inebriated and her head too dizzy, and cried again, but the giantess was reading a book. She cried herself to exhaustion, and laid on her back, staring at the ceiling with a blank expression.

Our heroes heated the end of the needle such that its sharp tip was red with heat. At the last minute, the mage, the businesswoman and the minotaur refused to go through with the ordeal. Our hero and the soldier bravely took the needle, climbed onto the baby's chest, leapt onto her face, and plunged the needle through her eye. The baby wailed even louder, but the giantess had arrived at a very good part of the novel.

When the giantess did answer the baby's pleas, she found the toy sheep scattered on the floor, impeding her entrance. She grabbed the lot of them and placed them on a nearby cabinet, not perceiving that our heroes clung to the undersides of these sheep. The giantess called the doctor; the doctor could do nothing for the baby's sight; the giantess now had the surprisingly fun task of ordering eyepatches for her daughter.

Our heroes rejoiced, though our heroines felt intense guilt. However, during their celebration, they had noticed the wyrm, who ate at the tree's roots and seemed content with gum, had climbed up and arrived into the palace, a worm compared to its inhabitants, and, after much looking around, aware of its inferiority, crawled and entered the daughter through an entrance, where the warmth would allow it to grow fat and birth its own young.

Though the baby had humiliated them, they endeavored to save her life. They climbed into the baby's closet and knocked down one of the coat hangers. Through great effort of their own they straightened the wire of the hanger into a single spear. They marched with the spear towards the baby's diaper, when the giantess entered the room, the eyepatch delivered same day.

She would have ended their lives had she not seen these ants try to speak. She put them to her ears, but found she could not hear them; she invented there a paper funnel in which their voices could be amplified. However, this did not work the other way around, and her voice was too loud to be understood, so she ingeniously used a toothpick to communicate with them.

Our heroes explained the situation to her, and so the mother, ignorant of any superior alternative, took the coat hanger and artfully, and with skill, and with patience that comes with being a mother, entered her daughter and fished out the wyrm. She kept the ants as her confidantes, and fed them very large pies, and gave them very large pitchers of mead, which, they lamented, the healer would have been very pleased with. She made beds out of her gloves and blankets out of her handkerchiefs, though it was very difficult to sleep, for something about the domestic setting caused a beast with two backs to appear, with the mage and minotaur conspicuously absent.

48

The giantess agreed to part with the golden goose, on the condition they were able to find her wedding ring. The ring had been discovered as being lost after she had done baking a pie; searching in her sugar and her flour she concluded she dropped it in the pie, which her husband had eaten in its entirety.

She clarified she only sought the ring to sell it. Her husband had fallen out of her favor, and she needed some allowance for herself and the child to start a new life.

Entrance was made easy by the giantess. She merely served her husband, late home that evening, after much gambling and drinking, his favorite dinner, pie. Unfortunately, he ate too quickly and spat our heroes upward into his nostrils, where they were quite lost. They thought they were going down; in fact they were going up; and made their way up the spinal cord to the brain.

The giant had woken up, wiped his face of crumbs, and found himself on the couch. He cured his hangovers in the way his father did: by slapping his skull. This set our heroes trembling, and they held onto the brain by driving stakes into it.

The giant, who followed this remedy with another, grabbed for a bottle of beer, but felt he had no desire to drink. He was lost as to why he did not want the beer in his hand that he often used to cure his alcoholism. He instead drank the remaining coffee his wife left in the pot before she went to work, and did not clean up after as he was eager to start dicing, for men diced even in the land of the giants.

As he made his way to the dicing man, our heroes argued over where to go. The mage, frustrated with her companions, carved a map of the human body on the giant's brain.

The giant, in a daze, bumped into a stall of fruits. Because he was not at heart a bad man, he apologized and picked them up. He discovered he was able to juggle them well, and had twelve fruit in the air at once. He noticed several lovely girls staring at his ability with adoration.

Strangely, he felt nothing for their glances, as our heroes decided then to have a midmorning meal of the grey matter. He instead observed the attention of several lovely boys.

He had gotten one of them on his knees and taken off his pants when the soldier had burned the patty, and had to cook another. He then, in a fit of passion, got on his own knees and gave the boy pleasure. The smell of the seed aroused the mage and the minotaur, and they made love again; the others gave them no heed.

So much seed was swallowed that, when they made their way to the lungs, they encountered many and decided to tame them, which involved slaying some. The smoke produced from a few fireballs made the giant feel dizzy, and upon visiting a doctor was diagnosed a kind of cancer. The giant wept; the doctor said, Fret not; science is much advanced, and the cancer is still in its earliest stage. The giant underwent surgery; he was promptly cured; he showed the bill of health to his wife, who was a gracious enough woman to prepare him his favorite meal, raw oysters. The oysters were not too pleased to be eaten alive, and chased our heroes into the esophagus.

The giantess was so grateful that she got on her knees and pleasured the giant, who had regained his prior lascivious nature. The resulting jolt in his spine scattered our heroes about the stomach.

49

Our hero awoke on an empty galleon. He saw a presence on the ship's deck. He tried to tap on the man's shoulder, but he found his hand passed through him.

The ghost explained he was once the captain of this vessel. In his life he had committed himself to a life of adventure and constantly pursued treasure and virgins to plunder. However, he and his crew were scooped up by the giant when he had acquired a mighty thirst during a camping trip, sailed through the esophagus as our hero did, and without any words died trapped in the giant's gut. His spirit however stayed on this earth, as he longed to see the vast blue sea again. Our hero despaired he too would die in the giant's stomach.

On Pie Island, the mage and the minotaur made love several times, then made up their minds to defy the businesswoman and leave. They launched several fireballs at the giant's stomach, to no avail.

His stomach inflamed, the giant found he could not produce stools as easily. He consulted his wife, who blamed his diet, and recommended a diet of leafy greens and legumes.

Considerable winds were produced in the giant, and the pirates rejoiced, setting sail. They picked up the mage and the minotaur on Pie Island, and promised to find the businesswoman and the soldier before they descended into the whirlpool of the rectum.

Our hero asked if they had seen an island made only of diamond. The pirate did not.

They fought many a tapeworm, from the giant's fondness of undercooked pork. The worms wriggled and writhed, smashed through the ship's planks, but our heroes valiantly repulsed them. The giant was pleased to no longer have chronic diarrhea.

They fought many a fluke, from the giant's preference for sashimi. They clung to the ship's sides, slowing it down, and had to be burned. The giant was pleased to be dispelled of his anemia, but not so pleased that he had no more excuses from joining his wife's jog.

They encountered many giardia, from a turd the giant swallowed in college. The giardia got along well with the sperm, and the businesswoman, whom they found on Candy Rock, taught them viral marketing, so the giant had to live with his bloody stools.

On the Herring Strait they found the soldier. He was enduring the stench of the harpies, was cut into pieces between Scylla's teeth, his testicles were crushed by the kraken, and thus he seemed to be having a good time. After parting with his friends, he relayed a brilliant white flash in the horizon he would see at night – the giant had swallowed a firefly, same camping trip – which could be the diamond ring.

They sailed to the diamond ring, which arose, pure, white, and shining, out of the horizon. To their greater surprise, they discovered a kingdom of normally-sized people living there, for the giant mistook their acropolis for a potato chip. These people would have been overly joyed to see guests, were they not mourning the upcoming sacrifice of their princess to a sea god. When they were informed the sea was a giant's gut and their god but the giantess's goldfish, they remained unconvinced and grieving.

The time of sacrifice drew near. The princess quivered in her iron-cold chains, bound to rocks. The seas churned, and the sea god emerged, devouring the princess in one gulp. Only, the princess was no princess, but the soldier, who limbed his way into the goldfish's brain to pilot it.

The people of the kingdom rejoiced, and agreed to our hero's plan to lash their kingdom, being the giantess's ring, to the sea god and their fleet of sperm and giardia. They all descended into the rectum.

50

Our heroes plunged into the small intestine, and began making the long and winded way to the rectum. Unfortunately, the walls of the small intestine absorbed some poor souls; they tried to pull them out, found themselves pulled in, and were passed through various layers of tissue, broken down part by part, until not even their bones remained.

Fortunately the mage and the minotaur had cast a spell that separated their souls from their bodies. They inhabited the bloodstream weakly, and held onto red blood cells to make their way to the bladder. They were fortunate the diamond, being truly unbreakable, was indigestible and went incidentally their path. Unfortunately, the body mustered white blood cells to stop them. They arrived in their skiffs, spears bared, and found spirits could not be pierced by weapons. They consulted an exorcist, who instructed them to pray, which prayer unfortunately worked, and many of them were slain. Yet even as a spirit the soldier could not be vanquished by thoughts and prayers and protected the lot of them.

The giant perceived his wife had become distant of late, or rather, relatively distant compared to the immeasurable gulf that had opened during the course of their marriage. She did not reveal her concern for our heroes. Overwhelmed now by powerlessness and loneliness, he walked the streets alone, and found a woman standing in the corner. They warmed to one another, and their lovemaking produced great rains, great winds, and great earthquakes in the lands below, for it had been a long time since he had his rocks off. On the following day he visited his doctor, who told him he now had a truly incurable disease.

The white blood cells felt undercompensated for their enforcement against our heroes, and instead of protesting or unionizing, chose to rebel against the body government itself, thus allowing our heroes free passage to the bladder, where they arrived into the testes and rebirthed themselves through the giant's abundant seed.

The doctor's dire diagnosis drove the giant to despair. He had always seen himself as strong and resilient, able to drive through any obstacle. Faced with this crisis, he felt the best thing to do, for his happiness and his family's, was to kill himself, his wife and his child. Who understands the darkness in man's mind?

To that end, he adopted his best behavior that evening. He cooked his wife dinner, relieved her stress, and intended to make love to her, thus giving her the life-extinguishing disease he had contracted. Inside the bureau was a knife he would dig into his daughter's heart.

As his wife freshened herself in the bathroom, he sat on the edge of the bed, staring at his hands, staring at the organ, erect, that had caused him so much misery now and in the past. He wanted to weep, but he could not be persuaded from his dark deed.

This is when our heroes began pushing the diamond out.

The giant was a hearty man and did not feel pain easily, and his depression had numbed him even more, but he felt a tight pinch in his genitals for quite some time. As he stared at his member, he noticed a large bulge at its base. Touching it, it was hard, much harder than the tumescent flesh. When it began moving, he was taken aback. It traveled and traveled all the way to his urethra, where it struggled to exit. The pain now, intensified by the stiffening of his member, and his confusion over the sexual stimulus, was so immense he was stunned and could not stop the diamond's breaking out.

Our heroes pushed and pushed, increasing the size of the urethra's slit more and more. However much strength they exerted, it would not come out. They heard behind them a rumble, then the sound of a dam breaking. The giant closed his eyes, his mind became black. Out came gushing from the urethra was a flood, a diamond ring, our heroes and all.

Our heroes celebrated, covered in white. The mage and the minotaur, whose passion was tempered by a cooler female side, reconfirmed their love for the other and vowed to be with the other forever. Unfortunately, the giant's member detumesced, crushing the minotaur beneath the stretched urethra.

The giantess and the giant confessed. She confessed her desire to leave him, and he confessed his recent infidelity and illness to her. He, realizing the preciousness of life from his illness, promised to live a healthier life and to be a better husband to her. Because he had made many promises before and broken just as many, she accepted him, for it did not hurt to have just one more broken promise.

The giantess awarded our heroes the golden goose, and they and the people of the sea descended down the tree, where they were received as heroes by all but one. The dryad pretended life would go on as it had before. It could not. She was put in jail for manslaughter, where she was fortunately spared many rapes for one good reason.

The citizens agreed to fight the giant's illness, in the hope he can live a normal life. When they were warned the war would be eternal, they rejoiced: that meant they would be paid forever.

Our hero returned to the doe and baby dragon, to whom he told about all of his adventures. She was merely glad to see him again.

51

There was yet one misfortune for our heroes upon returning to the land beneath the clouds, one that overshadowed all of their fortunes.

When our hero and the businesswoman returned to their farm, the guard did not welcome them. Confused, they also found the workers did not greet them. When they arrived to their office, they found the demon lord in their seat. He had bought out the farm.

Our hero retorted it was not possible, as they did not sell it. This distinction did not matter. The demon lord proved he had bought the land from the city, renegotiated the employees' contracts, and purchased the majority of the stock. In effect, the business was his.

And there were still no flowers.

The businesswoman was distraught and wandered aimlessly. Their acquaintances too were upset and scattered. Our hero was more resilient. He was also sad, but his sadness was lessened by the fact that he was alive. There were many instances in his new life when he should not have been.

Our hero spent many days with the doe, walked with her, ate many good meals with her, and contemplated on the day and night. One morning he told her he did not love her. She agreed. He told her, however, he wanted to still take care of her. He desired to take the business back and had a plan for it. He sought out his adventuring companions to aid him.

The people of the sea, having long been used to their isle, had sailed far and found an island just like the diamond ring and settled there. They encouraged the soldier to marry the princess; now the soldier was a prince, and even more, a general.

Our hero was welcomed lavishly by the people of the sea. These beautiful men and women served him all kinds of cuisine, and dressed him in the richest of garbs. He slept in the finest of beds, and was given the most attention of anyone. The princess was a beautiful girl and demonstrated that her virtues were as great as her beauty, by treating our hero with the greatest of grace and courtesy.

These were the qualities the soldier hated. He was a rugged man and hated parties; he was a crude man and hated court intrigue; he was a fighter, he did not like telling people how to fight; the kingdom was too peaceful; worst of all, he saw the princess more as a daughter than a lover. Now, the mermaids of the sea, these were fine lovers, and he would chase after them, they would laugh and insult him, he would catch them, take them to his private collection, use his carving knife to widen their anuses, then make love to them away from the princess's eyes, for he did not much care for his infidelity. He furthermore did not like eating fish every day.

He admitted to our hero he attempted to kill himself innumerable times. He gutted himself, but his guts stayed in place, holding the line; he drowned himself, but the water feared entering his lungs; he burned himself, but the fire jumped away; he poisoned himself, but it left his body without a word. In short, he was the best soldier, and the unhappiest kind of husband.

Our hero conceived a plan. The princess had many sisters, and he was able to acquire one of their clothes. He had the soldier dress as one of them, snuck out of the palace and was confronted by the guards of the dock, who disallowed all ships from entering and exiting at night save the royalty's. Our hero insisted he loved this princess; they were to elope on the mainland; the king would not be devastated, as he had many daughters.

The guards agreed, but they were wise. They asked our hero to prove his love. To our hero's chagrin, he set aside the soldier's skirt, removed his own pants, and to the best of his ability made love to the soldier, with feeling. This display of passion moved the guards, and they allowed them to board a small, stealthy skiff.

Yet on the skiff, from his recent experience, the soldier made a confession: he did not love the princess, but he did love her brother, the prince.

52

The soldier admitted that he had been compelled to hide his feelings for men in the army, so that he had not developed himself up to this point.

However, the prince was only attracted to the opposite gender.

Though the soldier had not developed his feelings on sexuality and gender, and our hero himself had zero experience with sexuality and gender, they concluded to respect the prince's sexual orientation. However, they reasoned that if he were a woman, he would prefer men.

Late into the night, our hero and the soldier bound the prince with rope while he slept. Our hero produced a scissor, and cut off the prince's manhood, thus making him, in his mind, a woman.

However, the prince was becoming faint of blood, thus they collected the blood from the wound in cups and had him drink it. Unfortunately this did not help and he expired. They cursed their ignorance and wished the mage had been there.

Luckily, the prince had many, identical brothers.

They resorted to a hypnotist to persuade the prince he was female. Unfortunately he had been raised a certain way, with a limited range of thinking, and concluded what our heroes had convinced him, that it was necessary to remove his manhood, the act concluding as it did for the last prince. They cursed their ignorance and wished the businesswoman had been there.

They resorted to the law and argued that the prince should be recognized as female. Unfortunately he would then be removed from his inheritance, and in sadness he removed himself from life by removing his manhood, incidentally. They cursed their ignorance and wished the minotaur had been there.

They resorted to taking the first prince's phallus and attaching it to a princess, so she would be male. Unfortunately their sewing was very poor, and she died of shock. They cursed their ignorance and wished the healer had been there, though they much agreed he was an asshole.

They resorted to taking a princess's womanhood and sewing it to a prince's rear, which reflected an evolution in their thinking that the male and female genders could not be described as an abundance of and a lack of, and that they could possibly coexist equally in various quantities. However, I do not need to say more except that this did not work.

They concluded that they needed different people of different skills and backgrounds to accomplish insurmountable goals.

Unfortunately there was only one prince left.

During these events our hero took pity on the princess. She much adored the soldier in spite of his recent distance. This gave our hero an ingenious idea. He relayed the dilemma to the princess and she agreed to the solution.

The soldier was gloomy from the frequency of his failures. Our hero encouraged him to visit his private collection. In the soldier's private collection awaited the princess, dressed in her late brother's garbs. The soldier was seized with passion and held the princess ardently, as he was a lusty fighter through and through.

Unfortunately for him, he had gotten too close to the tank of mermaids, who had bided their time until now. They leapt from the tank, grappled the soldier, and removed his manhood, for the act of tarnishing their womanhood. To their surprise, the blood from the wound did not come out, for soldiers do not leave a fortified position unless on their superior's orders.

Thus, in the eyes of the soldier, his wife, our hero, the island, and thus to the eyes of the world, and, mind, not in the eyes of the narrator, the soldier was now female, and the princess often made love to him with her brother's phallus strapped to a leather belt. The last brother mourned his brothers' deaths, but he was glad to keep his life and his manhood. The king was somewhat sad to see so many sons go, but he was glad to avoid civil war. To celebrate, the kingdom cut the mermaids' fish halves and served them as meals, for these were delicacies. To thank the mermaids, the princess allowed them her deceased brothers' lower halves. Thus everyone was pleased, the soldier was now a princess, and, as he was no longer a threat to the king, no longer being a man, he was given leave to plunder and conquer for his kingdom.

53

The businesswoman wisely hid her hoard of treasure, accumulated throughout the years. She had hidden them deep in a canyon and wrote a number of ciphers to recall its precise location, but a few knocks in the head in their previous adventures had caused her to lose it. She cursed her luck, gained a bit of weight, and lost every desire to adventure or continue any business.

As the mage was the closest to the businesswoman, our hero and the soldier approached the mage, who had used her riches to buy the former necromancer's castle. Unfortunately, the mage was in a foul mood, and ordered the former necromancer's skeletons to attack on sight. Though the soldier received their blades courageously, they were unable to get closer to the castle.

Our hero returned to the healer's former home. Hidden there was a sword blessed a long time ago by the healer's god of humanity, which would return souls to their proper shape and body. The healer had forgotten it after many nights with whiskey. Unfortunately the sword had lost the blessing long ago; it could be empowered again if a saint blessed it.

Our hero descended down the king's, who preceded the replacement, who preceded his replacement, who preceded the current parliament, mausoleum to determine which of the king's ancestors were saints. This did not please the goblins, who had migrated there after the stench left, and recollected the atrocities committed to their kind.

Our hero chose the most reasonable choice presented to

him: apologize, and offer any reparations the goblins desired. He returned back to them their possessions, including the deceased goblin chief's staff, except for those that were already sold, and directed them to the site of the last tribe's dying, so they could properly bury them. They believed in our hero's sincerity and accepted the apology, and aided him in crossing over the river of slime, passing the Cerberus, and entering the mausoleum.

Only one thing: our hero kept the brooch that belonged to the deceased goblins. He wished to give it to the businesswoman.

The preservation of the mausoleum was the result of an ancient magic involving the consecrated corpse of a saint, a beautiful woman who performed magic without magical intervention, and preserved her virginity to her death. Her tomb was sealed from the kings'; as the kings were now inanimate, having sated themselves through our hero, it was safe to reveal this woman to open air. The goblins had created an explosive using bladders of their flatulence, and created an opening into the tomb.

Our hero alone went forth with the sword and inspected the saint, not decayed whatsoever, in fact the same as when she died, and seemed to live still.

Our hero had taken out the sword for blessing when he heard shouting: the goblins saw a very dangerous parasite roaming around, and it was urgent that they inspect our hero's body in case he was already invaded. Our hero protested; the goblins asserted this was life-or-death; they approached; our hero hid the brooch in a certain hidden place of the saint, and allowed the goblins to strip him to their satisfaction and allow him to continue in privacy.

Our hero donned his clothing again and pulled the brooch out. The brooch was wet, and moreover liquid erupted from the saint, staining his clothes. He attempted to bless the sword, but the saint, now, was no longer a saint.

As he cursed his luck, the room became colder, and the spirit of the saint appeared. She thanked him for allowing her an experience more divine than any revelation, and sought to help him however she could.

Our hero and the saint agreed to create another saint. To become a saint, one had to be human, pure, blessed by the gods, and capable of performing miracles.

They sought the recruiter for someone matching this description; he was able to identify one. A man who had lost his limbs, his tongue and his genitals in several misfortunes, was a virgin and abstained from many acts others partook in, for reasons, thus fulfilling the first two requirements. Clearly, however, he was not blessed by the gods.

They considered giving all his wealth to charities, though his wealth only consisted of stale bread and a diaper.

They considered making him a martyr, but he had no hands to crucify.

It was also unfortunate that he was unable to speak in tongues.

They persuaded the man to clean people's feet, the poor and the wealthy's alike, by putting a washing cloth in his mouth. He asked for recompense. By nature of the task, they could not compensate him, but he would be richly rewarded in the thereafter. This was more or less satisfactory to him as he was not doing much in the now.

Unfortunately this path would have taken too long. Our hero asked the saint how it was she knew she was blessed. She responded that she had walked through a field of fire safely.

Our hero asked the sisters, who referred him to the dryad. The dryad did not mind the solitude of the jail, as she had lived her entire life alone, and so did not resent our hero all too much. She conjured a deadly disease that would eat the flesh of humans the instant it spread through the air. Our hero gave it to the man.

The man was asked to crawl through the marketplace. He did so. Though every organ of his ached with pain and his flesh was set afire, he did not die, as, dying, he would have spread the disease to his fellow man. Thus, it was proven he was blessed.

Our hero asked what miracles the saint performed. She replied that she cured an incurable disease in a girl and gave a prayer that allowed an army to win a war. There were no girls with incurable diseases that they particularly wanted to cure.

The people of the city were at arms against the people of the desert once more. The two armies confronted one another, the citizens standing before the walls, the desert people defending the walls.

It was at this time our hero brought the saint-in-training. Due to the violence of his illness all food melted as soon as it entered him, gave him no nutrients, and generated great bursts of gas. Our hero had fed him greatly prior to the battle, and as soon as the trumpets of war were sounded, his trumpet was sounded, thundering and collapsing the greatest of the walls. The city folk sacked the desert people's home; thus, the man was a saint.

The former saint, having done her work, departed to heaven, where, with disappointment, she found she was disallowed putting brooches inside of herself.

Our hero took the sword and put it through the saint; it

came out blessed. However, when the sword was appraised, it was revealed it was not blessed by the god of humanity, but an altogether new deity of recent creation: the god of gas.

55

The soldier wielded the holy sword before the mage's army of undead. Every swing brought out new sensations in these beings who had long ceased feeling. Every bone solely comprising their body desired to release gas, they convulsed violently, they yearned to release gas that they created new holes to eject dust, and then fell apart. Our heroes made their way easily to the mage's throne room.

The mage was wise, however, and erected a magical barrier no kind of magic could penetrate. She explained that the death of her husband three times and their divorce twice caused her such immense grief that she no longer desired to feel human emotions. Scorning the concept of afterlife and reincarnation, she was now undergoing the process of separating her soul from her body and tethering her soul to the physical realm by making her body into a magic artifact, thus becoming a lich. She would observe the world indifferently, until her body is destroyed or the destruction of the world itself. Our heroes could do nothing to stop her.

Just as she intended to sever the connection to her body, however, she felt a kick inside of her belly. She was pregnant with the minotaur's child. She had thrown away her life carelessly, and now she must live for an eternity knowing how foolish she was. She entered the great river of souls, her body stiff on her throne, undergoing its long transformation into nonbeing.

Our hero felt despair, but the soldier, ever a great fighter, lost no hope and prayed. He smelled something in the air. His god had answered him, with the scent of the mage's soul's flatulence.

Our heroes, using the holy sword as a guide and as the wind to their sails, entered the river of souls, guided only by the mage's scent. Here souls were divided into their various afterlives, and some were reborn into other worlds by many different goddesses. They were all very lovely, but our hero's was still the loveliest.

Their journey led them to the court of a yellow king, who was but a great length of golden thread wrapped around a skull encrusted with jewels. The king laughed; since the beginning of time he had consumed the souls of fledgling necromancers like the mage's, those who were foolish enough to give up their individual lives and stray from the river of souls. He had grown strong enough to challenge the gods themselves. There was no choice for our heroes but to return back.

The soldier was not daunted; he pointed his holy blade at the king; the king glared, summoning a great lightning bolt at the soldier; he leapt, and cut the king with his sword. The skull violently shook; he tried to suppress his urges; he cried, he had not cried for millennia; a very loud sound erupted from all of his cavities, and every soul he had eaten was freed. He himself was so embarrassed he subsequently died.

Our heroes guided the mage back to her body, reuniting her soul's flatulence to her body's. Upon returning, the mage took her staff, and broke it. She swore to renounce necromancy and to honor life, for her and her child's sake.

56

The mage swore never to use necromancy again, and thus could not use it to rediscover the ciphers in the businesswoman's mind. She recommended they instead revisit the places in the businesswoman's memory, so as to jog it. The businesswoman was initially reluctant, as she had much sleeping to do, but she was eventually convinced.

Our heroes visited the brothel our hero had briefly worked in, the mansion our hero's drug laundering was paying for, the Adventurer's Guild, the alley in which the businesswoman first met our hero and the auction room where the businesswoman tried to sell our hero's brooch. None of these helped her recollect the ciphers. However, our hero had recalled that fairy's foot, the city's drug of choice, helped the teenager to recall things.

They sought a consumable quantity of fairy's foot, but found it was difficult to procure. The demon lord had outlawed recreational use of fairy's foot, arguing it was detrimental to the city's health. The parliament, who depended on his business, agreed, allowing its use only to alleviate extreme cases of pain. However, he encouraged the doctors in his employ, and indeed every doctor in the city belonged to him, to sell as much fairy's foot as possible. Great quantities of fairy's foot were sold, which entered the hands of dealers, who sold them for prices much higher than the market's. Furthermore, he diluted all sold fairy's foot, so the infirm paid great amounts of gold to alleviate their pain only briefly and in part; on some bored days, he would concentrate the fairy's foot, such that the delivered drug was far, far more potent than expected. Citizens lost their life savings, the poor lost their lives to the drug, and the demon lord laughed, for he thought it was very funny to profit off of the foolishness of other people.

The businesswoman did not consider herself a righteous person. She, however, was very irritated by the flimsiness of this scheme. She easily procured our hero a prescription due to his obesity, she easily proved the quantity of the actual active ingredient in the prescription was below the legal requirement, and she easily convinced any potential thief of the prescriptions that it was far more profitable to sell mermaid's scale, which could be made from rat excrement.

They found a quiet alleyway to take the drug; the businesswoman went first, then the mage, then the soldier, then our hero.

Our hero fell into a stupor, replaying his worst memories. He flew through his history with his father, his schoolmates, and his publisher, arriving at his most recent adventures in the new world. His memories did not cease at this present moment; instead it led him to a spark of light; which grew larger and larger, and hotter and hotter, until it became a sun. It was the demon lord, who used his vast powers to psychically link with our hero.

The demon lord cackled, arguing that any attempt of our hero's to defeat him was useless.

But he was not attempting to defeat him, he was merely trying to buy back his business.

"There have been countless of adventurers in the past, and I have defeated them all. I am invincible. I am a force of nature."

What was even the point of living then?

"All life needs food to sustain itself on. Man needs his various comforts to survive. Even the gods need prayer. But I, I do not require anything. I was created to be evil. All I do justifies my existence."

Our hero thought he needed to chill out, and offered his share of fairy's foot. The demon lord agreed, and when both were sufficiently mellowed out our hero asked if he could use his psychical powers to help the businesswoman, to which proposition he agreed.

57

Our hero and the demon lord encountered some difficulty leaving our hero's mind. They had to surpass our hero's bullies, his father, his high school gym teacher, and his editors, each empowered in proportion to how much our hero feared them, and he feared them greatly. The demon lord had met many adventurers, seduced many, gazed into many visions of the other world, and understood many of their fears, yet our hero had so many anxieties he was surprised, being an omnipotent being himself, how he could even stand in front of him. He attributed his survival to the stupid gods.

They defeated each of these psychical representations and found the entrance to the businesswoman's mind. She was dreaming of their office, which the demon lord had taken, working lovingly with a mysterious other. The demon lord had to use his immense powers to travel deeply into the businesswoman's memories; this would be routine work, but it would take long.

They discussed our hero's idea for a light novel. Of the many minds he raided, he had never heard of a light novel. He had heard about movies, he had heard about manga, he had heard about anime, yet this innovation never came to light. Our hero thought him a very poor man, living in a very poor world. The demon lord thought otherwise. What do these things matter in the face of evil? Our hero had no answer, but he thought light novels were really cool.

They talked about the plot. "What!" the demon lord protested, "this is a very weak demon lord to be defeated by a human being." But the hero did not win with sheer might alone; he won through the power of friendship and love. "I have fought many comrades, I have fought many lovers; friendship and love do not suffice." Yes, but the friendship and love in this hero was the greatest, so it did work. The demon lord could not refute this, though he tried, so he dismissed this as the dumbest thing he had ever heard.

And yet he did not let the subject go. He boasted about the many adventurers he had defeated. They could fill the oceans, he claimed. What was the thousand and first adventurer to him? Yes, but this adventurer was the hero of the story and thus the best. The demon lord concluded, no, *this* was the dumbest thing he had ever heard, it could never be true, and he hated our hero for suggesting it, but his mind was so obscured by the fairy's foot it did not occur to him he should abandon this enterprise.

They eventually arrived early in the businesswoman's memories, when she, as a teenager, joined the Thief's Guild. They discovered a secret among them where they used the guild's charter to encode messages. They found the cipher.

They made to leave the memory when they saw that the young businesswoman was propositioned by several boys to play strip poker. She notably seemed nervous, and went to the restroom, which the boys hovered around. This troubled our hero's conscience, and so he sought to play in place of the businesswoman, using the demon lord's powers to disguise himself.

He played very poorly and denuded himself. He seemed to be the only person who lost. On the next wager, the boys decided the loser would use their breasts to pleasure the winner of the pot, upon noticing our hero's magnificent breasts, more ample than the businesswoman's. The demon lord revealed he did not understand how his powers worked.

Our hero, predictably, lost, and acted as the loser ought to. He minded the smell of another man's seed, though he never minded his own. As he was blinded, he stumbled and fell, which the boys advantaged by groping what they had believed, in their prepubescence, was a girl's body. They stripped themselves of their pants, and intended to use our hero's hands. As our hero was not very dexterous, they felt no relief, and grabbed ahold of our hero's rear.

Our hero then let out a long wind. The boys became very limp, for reasons. In fact, this experience left such an impression on them that they suffered impotency and were mocked by their girlfriends for the rest of their lives.

To the young businesswoman's surprise, she saw only our hero when she left the restroom. She washed our hero's face, and offered him bread and beer. He agreed, and the memories ended there.

When they recovered from the drug's effects, our hero relayed this to the businesswoman in present time. She realized she did not use the guild's charter but the magazine in that restroom. She also, unbeknownst to her, lost her parsimony, brought upon her by the fear of her powerlessness, which our hero had cured.

This was the time our hero returned to her the brooch, which began their partnership. She thanked him, cherishing the gift.

When the demon lord recovered from the drug's effects, he thought it almost lamentable how the great heroes' lineage had run dry.

Then he cursed himself for not stealing the businesswoman's acumen.

58

The cipher revealed the specific locations along the canyon where the treasure was buried. Because it was vast, and because they desired to keep it secret, the four of them only transported it, piece by piece, into a different safe house.

As many of these assets were not currency, they agreed to sell them to a fence, who would make them liquid. However, the fence could not be of the city government, who did the bidding of the demon lord. They concluded the identity of their buyer: the demon lord, as he had the most wealth.

They passed the assets to the grandmother, who was hard of hearing and sense generally. As the grandmother was unable to travel very far, they used the crippled mailman, who was eager for sedatives for his injuries, as her emissary. The mailman, however, had no power to enter the demon lord's castle alone, so he was accompanied by our hero and the businesswoman. The demon lord found this so odd that he suspected nothing.

However, he found himself too busy to appraise the value of every individual piece the group offered to sell. They agreed on independent evaluators, who would be the dwarves, the creators of much of the treasure. As they were friends, the dwarves evaluated the worth of the treasure generously. The demon lord did not mind, as he possessed wealth lasting eternity. The exchange was made; our heroes were given more gold coins than could fill a palace.

They stored the gold with the goblins, whom our hero felt were trustworthy. Our heroes sought a plot of land to start their new venture. They went to speak to the officials of the city government without the businesswoman, who desired to ensure the correct number of gold pieces were exchanged.

Unfortunately the city officials reported that there were hardly any plots of land they could offer. A mysterious lobbyist argued passionately that, for the quality of living and the welfare of the people in the city, land needed to be certified and insured before purchasing, certified to have passed safety inspections and insured in the case disaster were to befall the owners of the land; he made his argument through many generous donations. These checks raised the value of land dramatically, such that the only true owner of land was, coincidentally, the demon lord.

Downcast, our heroes returned to their gold and the businesswoman, who, in their surprise, had grown several feet taller, had grown scales, a tail, sharp teeth and wings.

To the businesswoman's own surprise, she did not realize the cursed gold had made her a dragon either. However, what kept her from succumbing to the intense greed caused by the gold was the brooch our hero gave her. Besides, they would make several times the golds' worth once they invested it.

Our heroes relayed to her the city officials' news. This did not bother the businesswoman all too much. She suspected as much, and had planned to buy land from her own people, the folk of the desert.

59

The folk of the desert did not like the citizens of the former forest, but they were not prejudicial. To buy land, our heroes had to pass the trials of their god, who had formerly been represented by a certain blue-banded rock.

The ritual consisted of drinking from a bowl of a certain hallucinogen, then surviving the night under the supervision of the city's elders. This was the ritual before the god collapsed. Now, to mirror their god's descent to the underworld, the initiate had to wander through the desert, without food or water, and only return when they experienced ecstasy. Our hero went alone, for he had endured starvation once, and he was sure this time he would get abs.

By the end of the day he had been severely sunburned, and could barely walk on his burned feet, for he was very pale and knew very little about the power of the sun in his mother's basement. He had tried to drink water from a cactus, but was only pierced; he had tried to eat the buzzards who chased him, but they danced around him; he had been stung by a scorpion, whose eggs would urge out of his genitals; he had been bit by a cobra, whose venom gave him diarrhea; now it was night, and he would surely freeze on the cold, white sands.

What he feared most was the demon lord's criticism of his light novel. Maybe he made it too easy for the hero to defeat the demon lord. He conceived of an idea where the heroine would be hypnotized by the demon lord and betray the hero in a black leather bikini. He would spend half the novel trying to get her to her senses through the power of love.

Just before our hero's eyes closed from exhaustion, and his breathing his last breath, he saw in the horizon, beneath the great white moon, a shining object running toward him, majestic in the moonlight.

The creature had the head of a baboon, and the crest of a lion. Its four feet were the claws of a rooster, and its tail was that of a rabbit's. It had the wings of a quail, the plumage of a peacock, and the ridges and scales of a salamander. Its most prominent fin resembled a catfish's, and its secondary fin resembled a dolphin's. Its mouth resembled a bear's, one eye that of a rat, the other eye of an otter's, the third eye of a moose's. A blowhole was in the center of the cranium. Its tongue was forked like a snake's. It was spotted like a leopard.

The bogwent took pity on our hero, for, like our hero, he was orphaned from the forest upon its destruction. He spat on our hero, staunching his wounds, for the spit of a bogwent had curative properties.

He then brought our hero on his back and returned him to the folk of the desert. The folk of the desert accepted our hero's story, which by appearance seemed like the story of their god's, which was really the story of our hero's hero in his light novel.

However, when it came time for our heroes to purchase the land, the folk of the desert were told the city had issued an order to stop all exports, supported by a mysterious lobbyist, so as not to support their enemies. This meant our heroes' gold was nearly valueless. Our heroes proposed: they would melt the gold and create a statue of their god, the dwarves being the sculptors. The folk of the desert liked this idea, yet after centuries of worship they could not agree on what their god actually looked like.

At the last, they agreed: as our hero had the most recent vision of their god, they would use his design. Thus, on one of the many worlds across existence, there is one statue of Yusuke Kyusuke and yet in none of the worlds is there one word written about him.

Our heroes now were able to build their casino.

60

The demon lord did not lie to our hero. As an incarnation of the concept of evil itself, he had no need to sleep or eat. In the night time, when there was relatively little activity in the lands, he merely sat in his throne room, waiting for adventurers to come to try to defeat him.

In the morning, he decided to visit the casino which had recently opened in the desert. It was a lavish palace, whose columns and towers were made of pure gold, or were cleverly designed to convince others they were in their entirety. It overlooked the sea, which itself glittered like gold when the sun cast its happy rays of light on its surface. A boardwalk had been erected over the sea, so that patrons sunned on the sand or swam in the waters.

The casino hosted a great variety of games, none of them dicing. Patrons played blackjack, craps, and roulette, all games our hero remembered in his past life and whose rules he very poorly reproduced. These games were operated by goblins, who were happy to be employed; they also operated the slot machines, which consisted of them spinning three wheels whenever a patron prompted them to.

The forest folk, who looked more and more human every day, maintained the facilities and operated the restaurants, which served fine cuisine. The Adventurer's Guild acted as security.

The casino also hosted several different forms of entertainment. The mage and the god of fire performed stage magic, the sisters did acrobatics, and music was performed by the recruiter, the tailor, the mailman and the cuckold, who felt bad for the mailman's face.

Outside of the casino was a very different story. The workers were undercompensated and struggled to make ends meet. They released their tension by smoking and drinking, and some of them gave away their hard-earned money to women in the form of prostitution and pornography. They encouraged dog-fighting, and placed bets on the dogs; though the dogs were willing fighters, they did not appreciate being treated so cheaply. Everyone had a gun beneath their pillow, everyone had bars over their windows, and behind every wall were the feces of insects, particularly the walls of the children's bedrooms. In short, they had lost their sense of humanity in the pursuit of a paycheck.

These sad living quarters were visited frequently by men who had lost everything to the casino. They begged for money, for food, for a means to go home, though few wanted to return home to tell their wives and children they had lost their savings and their homes as a result of their weaker selves. Presented with the option to confront the truth, they instead drowned their senses in mermaid's scale, of which formidable gangs had developed around the casino to possess the privilege of selling. The casino, in truth, thought this was a fortuitous development, as the weaker their patrons' senses, and thus the weaker their thoughts, the more they gambled and the more money they gave over.

These savage scenes would have upset the desert folk, who believed ardently for their god, had the casino not brought them a great deal of wealth.

The demon lord considered the intense contradictions that

were raised by the casino's inception, the overwhelming luster of wealth and the seeming happiness it could buy versus the inequalities caused by that wealth and the human lives that wealth exploited, juxtaposed in front of the complete lack of value that wealth generated except in soothing the softer parts of the human soul, and realized he wanted to possess it.

He spoke with the folk of the desert, and participated in their ritual. Using his awesome powers, he was able to impersonate their god, commanding them to sell the plot of land the casino sat on to the demon lord. The folk of the desert agreed; sun set down; sun set up; the demon lord still did not own the casino; he inquired after it; the folk of the desert considered their bank accounts, and decided their god misspoke.

The demon lord resumed the guise of their god, labeling our heroes as heretics, and ordered the desert folk to slaughter them. The desert folk reconvened; "heretic" was a very harsh word.

The demon lord tried once more, insisting disaster would befall the desert folk the longer our heroes occupied the land. The desert folk reconvened; they believed the disaster was metaphorical, and, if it was not, it was their fate to endure it, and prayed for their god's mercy.

The demon lord, once more, in the guise of their god, revealed to his followers that our heroes undervalued their stock in the casino significantly. The desert folk were incensed and fought the casino's guards. Surpassing them, they were confronted by very beautiful women, who offered them free credit for the casino's games. They accepted this, and put down their arms. Seeing this, the demon lord abandoned his current plans.

At this time, our hero approached the demon lord with a contract: the casino would buy stock selectively from the demon lord's farm, for a reduced price and in certain quantities. The demon lord was suspicious, and assumed our hero had a sinister plot for him; our hero rebutted he would only speak through a lawyer; the demon lord, incensed by his standoffishness, accepted the lucrative contract.

The casino bought much of the farm's stock; the casino and the farm became quite profitable; the casino bought more stock in greater quantities, demanding more exclusive discounting; the casino raised the farm's competitors, threatening to take their business elsewhere; soon the farm was more beholden to the casino. The demon lord swore to destroy the casino, as he had destroyed countless of adventurers in the past.

61

The demon lord defeated the casino's guards and stormed our heroes' office. His head burst in a blinding light, and he bit them, transforming them into vampires.

Unfortunately, their vampiric state allowed them to stay up at night, accomplishing more work in a day. They did not mind drinking blood, though the mage was a vegan, in honor of her late husband; she drank beet juice. Furthermore, they anticipated an attack by the demon lord and summoned their army of lawyers, who, though the demon lord was accused only of assault, painted him as a villain, an idiot, a pederast and a bedwetter. Though the demon lord suffered no physical harm, and was given a minimal fine, the reputational damage was vast, and his workers began to migrate to the casino.

The demon lord then relied on his dominance over all vampires, commanding our heroes to obey him. Our heroes had also anticipated this, and had put a clause in their employment that, in the case of mental unfitness to perform their duties, the ownership of the company would be transferred to the casino's manager. The demon lord had no choice but to make this individual, too, a vampire.

Now the whole casino's workforce was comprised of vampires. Even after going through these lengths, the demon lord did not fully own the casino, as its stock was divided by anonymous stockholders. When the demon lord tried to dictate the casino's operations, the investors were more often than not displeased, thus sold their stock, thus leaving the casino in a more fraught state than it was found in. Worse, as all the employees were vampires, they bothered his solitude at night in his throne room, usually with very trivial matters of the casino's operations.

The demon lord exchanged guts with the businesswoman, hoping to acquire her intuition. Unfortunately, because she had the build of a dragon, she was able to install an alarm in her gut and her mind, which triggered; a company of lawyers arrived, and demanded he return the gut to its rightful owner or go to jail. He returned the gut back.

He relinquished the businesswoman's thrall and proposed for her to operate the casino while he reaped its pleasures. She only wished to speak to her lawyer, who sued the demon lord for unlawfully entering her client's mind without permission. Scoffing, the demon lord thought this was a trifle, until he found, after the recent sale of the businesswoman's treasure, the lawsuit would cost him all of his remaining wealth. He considered making vampires of the casino's lawyers or the city's government, yet thralldom only worked when he was present. He relinquished control of the casino's workers and settled out of court for half of his remaining treasure.

Shortly after, the demon lord found always a number of his crops perishing. When he inspected a withered tomato, he saw bite marks from very large canine teeth. The casino workers had turned the vegetables into vampires at night, while he was busy awaiting adventurers in his throne room. Furthermore, the beef they had sold recently tasted dry and stale; the casino had converted his cattle into vampires as well.

Incensed, he sought to kill everyone in the casino, yet, as

vampire children can sense the presence of their parent, they were very well-equipped to hide from him. The demon lord paid vampire hunters very handsomely to kill them.

Unfortunately the vampire hunters' business was very transparent and the casino's lawyers caught wind of the fact that their clients had died. The demon lord was forced to resurrect the casino workers, curing them of their vampirism, and to recompensate them for the duration of their deaths and more.

The demon lord was now running out of money.

62

The demon lord was involved in several very expensive lawsuits.

One of his workers sued him for a lack of workplace protections. This worker did not belong to the farm. This was a goblin who defended his castle from a group of adventurers some centuries ago. The demon lord had dismissively called him "fodder", expected him to be slain by the adventurers for the benefit of making his castle appear more fortified, then made him into an undead abomination for his eternal servitude with no compensation whatsoever. The demon lord was forced to settle out of court.

A nobleman sued him for defrauding him on the value of his castle for the sake of a loan; the demon lord insisted the castle had several mummies, he only had one; the castle supposedly had a spike trap, but it was only for mice; one of the rooms in the castle supposedly was large enough for a dragon, it could only fit a garden variety snake; and the demon lord ultimately stole the money anyway, without paying interest. The demon lord was forced to settle out of court.

A woman accused the demon lord of penetrating her without consent. He insisted he did not; she pointed to the bite marks on her neck; he put her under his thrall; this did not help as she was a co-plaintiff. The other woman asserted that the demon lord had transformed into a demonic horse and impregnated the woman, creating her centaur child, whom she loved very much. The demon lord asserted there were no witnesses that full moon. The woman produced the owner of the inn who heard neighing, her best friend who recalled her account, one of the vampires of the demon lord's castle who recalled he was not at home that night, and the inn's stablemaster who asserted none of his horses could climb to the second story. The demon lord was forced to settle out of court, and was now called a horse fucker.

All of these plaintiffs were provided lawyers from the casino, and many of the laws were lobbied for by the casino, who were more than happy to ensure a fair, nondiscriminatory workplace for their employees.

Furthermore, the local newspaper, funded by the casino, reported all of the demon lord's misdeeds, which, he argued, were okay in the wild expanse that preceded the city when only the strongest ruled, such that his farmers became quite disgusted and joined the casino's entrepreneurial program to start their own farms.

Now the demon lord had very little money left. One of the casino's lawyers presented to him a deal to buy his dying farm. Incensed, the demon lord transformed into a wolf and tore the lawyer into shreds.

Now the demon lord had a dead body in his castle, and did not desire any more lawsuits.

63

The demon lord collected the approximately fifty pieces of the lawyer into a sack and sought for places to throw them in.

He found a lake, but feared the lady of the lake would be a witness.

He found a grove, but feared the treants would be witnesses.

He found an abandoned ruin, but feared the fisher king would be a witness.

He decided then to devour the corpse whole. He returned to his castle, where the city's police asked if he knew where the lawyer was. He asserted the lawyer visited, he received the deal, would think it over, and the lawyer left. He wondered why the police asked so.

The police then asked if they could analyze his stool. The demon lord thought this was very odd. The police explained this was merely procedure; a werewolf recently tried to disguise a murder by devouring his victim.

The demon lord felt twinges of fear as he squatted over the chamber pot. He recalled he had some vampire cows' meat in reserve. This gave him a plan. He ground the beef and served this to the police officers. They sampled the beef and found no traces of the lawyer in them. They thanked him for his time and departed.

The demon lord's accountant asked him where the vampiric beef was. The city sought accurate records of their stock, and he needed to ensure the books were properly calculated at penalty of a lawsuit. The demon lord panicked, and used his stool to replace the used beef. The accountant was satisfied and left.

The police officers returned to apologize to the demon lord once more, and to ask a separate set of questions. As it was late, the demon lord offered them dinner. One of his brides served them beef. To the demon lord's horror, he was served his stool. He was left with no other choice.

As the demon lord tasted the rancid "meat", the police officers explained that, based on the lawyer's schedule, the lawyer's last location was in this castle; the casino also required his physical copy of the deal. The deal in question was in the stool he was currently eating,

He explained that he threw the deal away. The police found this odd as, in his earlier account, he promised to consider it. The demon lord thought the deal was void with the lawyer's death. This was an unusual conclusion to make as the lawyer was merely an emissary. The demon lord, who was unused to laws of any kind, began to sweat.

He asked to be excused, and summoned the precise wording of the contract in his memories. Unfortunately, he was unable to replicate the writing style of the script.

He vomited the stool in his stomach, summoned the lawyer's spirit, placed it in the body of one of his minions and compelled it to rewrite the contract. He then delivered it to the police, apologizing for his mistaken memory. Unfortunately the paper was not of the same material as the casino's copy. The attorney general of the city gave him a summons.

He considered transporting himself and the castle far away to mull on his options. However, if he left, there was a possibility the police would seize the farm and sell it, allowing the casino to buy it. Though the farm was no longer profitable, the idea of selling it drove him mad with anger.

The demon lord sought a human vessel, placed the lawyer in them, and compelled him to tell the police he was alive and had been in an affair as an explanation for his absence. Unfortunately it was discovered the lawyer's body was, in fact, not his. The demon lord was sued for defrauding the lawyer of his body, and this time he could not settle out of court.

The city requested his castle. He now only had a farm and no money. Worse, he earned the reputation of a racist who thought all humans looked alike.

64

The demon lord considered killing every human, within the city and casino alike, and starting all over. This was his strategy in past days. Unfortunately, it was easier to start a new settlement in the past; he merely had to find the meanest human and set him as king. The republic was governed by various personalities that would be difficult to cultivate, and its institutions and businesses were led by minds given to various secrets passed down through the centuries. Therefore, he would have his castle back, true, but he would not be guaranteed a successful casino. And, most importantly, though he could take his time to cultivate these talents, his rage would subside by them, and at this point the value of possessing the casino was for vindication.

He felt his only option was to become the prime minister of the city's parliament. He replaced a candidate for a seat in the district; he pitched himself; his polling within the district was low; he murdered just enough constituents; he won the seat; unfortunately, because the district's population had dramatically decreased, he was conferred very little power in parliament, and the other members ignored him.

He then replaced the sitting official for the largest constituency; his constituents did not like him, nor his ideas to endow them with extraordinary powers, which had nothing to do with tariffs or the interest rate; he asked the spirit of the sitting official what to do; because the official was a decent man, he told the demon lord what to say, without anything in exchange; unfortunately increasing the rate of tariffs did not go very well with his constituents when the casino, a foreign entity, simply decided not to deal with the city any longer.

The demon lord no longer relied on the spirit. He instead resorted to the tactics of the asshole: he laid the fault of the problem squarely at the casino's feet, and urged his constituents to protest against the casino and its practices. This worked, and the constituents, though they were poorer, were unified and happy in their rage.

He attempted these tactics for the whole city. They were largely well-received; a minority disagreed. He put them in a correction camp.

He was poised to buy his castle back had the casino not bought it in order to renovate it as a haunted house attraction. The demon lord attempted to retract the deal, then to buy it back; he was too late.

It took some time to complete the haunted house attraction; many of its workers were migrants from the city, who had no work otherwise. When it was opened it was well-received. Unfortunately one of the migrant workers was found dead; soon thereafter, fairy's foot was found in his possession.

The demon lord was gleeful in being able to prosecute against the casino, after so many prosecutions were placed upon him. Unfortunately the casino's lawyers framed the issue as stemming from the city's drug epidemic, that the prime minister and his parliament refused to address. Public support plummeted; the parliamentary members conspired to vote out the demon lord; the demon lord, incensed, sought to weed out this issue. He tried to purchase the drug addiction out of the addicts of the city. He discovered the issue had biological as well as psychological origins. Thus he believed the easiest way to dispel of the problem was to kick out the addicts. Unfortunately the resulting grief of their friends, lovers and mothers in turn caused themselves to be addicts.

The demon lord encouraged the addicts to take a weaker drug, troll hair, but the addicts, to compensate for their dulled response to the drug from their overuse of fairy's foot, discovered a means to increase troll hair's potency dramatically. The demon lord cursed their ingenuity.

Due to the grief and misery of the city, many of the city's people began migrating to the casino, which had formed a kind of city; they were welcomed with open arms, as the casino had sensible immigration policy. Thus the demon lord's city was left only with drug addicts, who spent most of their earnings on drugs, and many of their working hours incapacitated by said drugs.

65

During these events, a newspaper had gotten into the habit of calling the demon lord many things, as "horse fucker", "man eater", "fraud", "broke", "and "moron". Though he was impersonating the prime minister of the city, he found it difficult to let this go, and personally assassinated the news writers. Unfortunately the newspaper continued writing, as the news writers were zealous in their mission and, more so, greatly enjoyed the casino's pay. The demon lord was incensed when they wrote him a new insult: "snowflake".

He hired a lawyer to handle the newspaper. He hated this lawyer, because the lawyer loved him; nevertheless, he found him useful.

In speaking to this lawyer, he realized it was easier to simply run as himself using the current crisis. As prime minister, the demon lord called a snap election; the demon lord ran as himself. His platform blamed the casino for causing the troll hair epidemic and stealing all the good workers because of their greed, and he proposed to wage war with the casino, as the city had often done in the past to redistribute wealth. This proposal went very well and he was elected, not unanimously until he burned the dissenting ballots.

Contrary to his own belief, the newspaper did not suddenly adulate him with his victory. Instead, they invented new nicknames for him, as "murderer", "warmonger", and "micropenis". It appears that they were not fond of war, as they were not warriors. The latter insult offended the demon lord all the more as he technically did not have a penis.

The demon lord announced martial law, though the state was not in any duress, and used his extraordinary powers to seize the newspaper's office and fill it with writers who were fond of him, and called him "great", "very smart", "awesome" and "well-endowed".

As the demon lord prepared for war, he noticed some graffiti outside of his office. He walked towards it and saw "dickless". Evidently, if writers cannot write on paper, walls were just as adequate.

The demon lord demanded the writers be killed. No one knew who they were. He set up spies in every corner of the city. Unfortunately this was very costly. He became accustomed to surveilling the city himself every day, and used magic to scry constantly. This became very tiring. The war kept getting delayed. New nicknames came up: "blowhard" and "scaredy cat".

When he awoke from a long slumber, his office was on fire. Despite his many powers, and in spite of his head being on fire, he was unable to put out fires. He screamed from his office for help; help arrived; he received a new nickname, "little girl".

In the aftermath, he discovered the casino had sent their own army to attack the city, killing few civilians and mostly destroying the city's stock. The demon lord was incensed and gave a very fine speech on how the city had to defend and avenge itself. The city cheered the defending part, but less for the avenging part. The writers now had new nicknames: "hypocrite" and "pussy".

The demon lord wondered why he was unable to assault

the casino immediately. The problem was that the people were not receptive to it. Why did he care what the citizens had to say? The citizens, as was reasoned, could simply not follow along, thus it were no different than if he carried out the initiative himself. Who would force them to do so? The police? The police were also citizens. This upset the demon lord greatly. Things had never been done this way. Alas, this was one of the flaws of a self-sustaining economy whose participants were not directly paid by the ruler.

To counter this, the demon lord destroyed the biggest plant for troll hair production, and pinned the blame on the casino, hoping to offend the citizens enough to avenge themselves. Instead, they were very happy about this and became healthier, and generally more loving of life.

The demon lord attempted to foment crises by destroying things the citizens loved. He destroyed the building of parliament. The citizens did not much like parliament.

He destroyed the stock market. The citizens did not much like insider trading.

He destroyed a monument to himself. The citizens did not like him.

He destroyed the forum, where many sold their wares, bought provisions, and generally joined and relaxed. This did upset them greatly, but they simply rebuilt it. Their energies, after reconstruction, were too exhausted for war. After all this, they did not trust the government all too much, only themselves.

The demon lord received a new nickname after this: "thin skinned".

66

Not only was the demon lord unable to litigate or wage war against the casino, his reputation suffered tremendously in these affairs. Never in the eternity he lived had he been called "loser", and he was unable to avenge himself for it. He was frustrated that, whenever he thought of a good solution, someone got in the way. His lawyer professed his inability to sue the casino; his parliament was unable to take action without the people's consent; the people paid them no mind, wanting to live their lives; the casino minded their own business and generated profit.

The demon lord realized, in this introspection, that the man given power by the citizens is not powerful; the man who can change the citizens' opinions, however, is. He decided himself to become a newspaper writer, setting up a proper replacement for prime minister. He found the man responsible for all the slander against him. To his surprise, the man was old, and not spry; he had lost a leg, not in a war, but to disease; he was rather disliked, as his choler was fit only for insulting people, and, indeed, that was all he was capable of doing, for slander was his hobby and calling in life, for he was given no talent in improving his own.

The demon lord sought to cooperate with this man. He gave the man money to change his mind; then he left.

When he discovered the man was still slandering his name, he realized that money only incentivized him to do what he did best, which was slandering him, the demon lord. He gave the man money to slander others, so as to set aside the attention that was currently reserved for him; then he left.

When he discovered his reputation was not improved, he realized that slander is, in effect, an infinite resource, that citizens never tired of consuming, and that even after all the slander, concerning, for example, parliament, businessmen, the woman who made pies, the writer's next door neighbor, who sang too early in the morning, they still had appetite left over for slander against the demon lord, which was the writer's best slander. In fact, the citizens hated the demon lord more, because they hated their fellow citizens more.

The demon lord was intrigued whether this dampened public participation and voting, and whether he could advantage from this consequence. This did not, as the citizens had nothing better to do.

He gave the man money to make up slander, as invasions that would not happen, disasters that would not fruit, corruption that sounded exciting, scandals that seemed evil and not banal; then he left.

He discovered, though the citizens enjoyed these lies, they were equally both too busy and too lazy about them. The writing simply made them more miserable.

The demon lord then decided to dispose of the writer by killing him and resurrecting him as a nightmare. The nightmare, at night, would dutifully take the dreams of a neighbor, and put it into the dreams of another neighbor; thus the citizens understood who was sleeping with their wives, stealing from their baskets, and calling them morons behind their backs. However, because these were dreams, none of the neighbors possessed proof. The citizens were angrier, the citizens were meaner, they had forgotten about the demon lord's most recent scandals, but they somehow possessed the idea that this was vaguely the demon lord's fault, which galled the demon lord, for, though they had no evidence, their assumption was correct.

The demon lord tried a different track. He gave the nightmare the body of a minion, and ordered him to write very flattering things about himself: that he was searching for new lands to colonize, that he was worth a billion gold coins, that he knew much about many things, that he enjoyed dicing, that he did not have alopecia, and that he was cool and with it.

It did not occur to the demon lord that people did not like him because he desired to be the center of attention.

Nevertheless, he did attract people with this approach. He attracted many individuals who had alopecia, knew far fewer things than he purported, and were not billionaires, and did not have the motivation or the wherewithal to acquire these things themselves and sought them in other people, in exempla the demon lord. These people did not amount to many votes.

67

Nevertheless, the demon lord sought what he could do with these followers. They were not very skilled, otherwise they would have busied themselves doing other things. They were weak-willed, otherwise they would have forged an identity separate from the demon lord's.

However, though they were not wealthy, they were willing to buy many things. They were neither able to acquire power nor virtue that led to happiness, so they were left with possessing the material things that people who were happy possessed, or people who were purportedly happy.

This worked very well for the demon lord. He sold them action figures, coins stamped with his image, that have no value, and other memorabilia, which allowed him to regain a significant proportion of his wealth. In exchange, they gave him their adulation, and vociferously defended him from all criticism. Both sides considered this a fair exchange.

He once had a dark army that could ravage any kingdom he desired, but this was a good consolation. He set these followers to work on his farm, and they did well, for they were neither bad nor entirely incompetent people. This gave him more gold.

The demon lord was now in a position to buy the castle again. He visited the haunted house, and was escorted by our hero to the businesswoman's office. To get to the office he had to go through the entire haunted house. This irked the demon lord, but he agreed nevertheless.

Our heroes had converted his lava pit into a steam room. Our heroes had recast the mummies from flesh-hungry monsters into a live in-house band. His vampiric brides took the ticket stubs from guests. His armies of undead were decorations for the thrill rides. Indeed, our hero was certain that they had to go through the tunnel of love to get to the office, where the succubi were seen repairing the ride. He was furious to discover the office was but a few feet from the entrance.

The demon lord made his proposal to the businesswoman. The businesswoman carefully considered it. She confessed that the haunted house was actually very profitable and a good addition to the casino as a kid-friendly alternative. It did not seem prudent to sell it just for liquid assets. She made this offer: purchase the haunted house, or, in his words, the castle, for all his current liquid assets, as well as the farm too.

The demon lord was incensed and refused. He offered to pay with more gold, though his followers were already deep in debt after purchasing a new collection of urban streetwear. But the businesswoman, very reasonably, did not need more liquid capital, as there was not much more she could buy; she did, however, need to develop some level of autonomy from her wholesalers, who occasionally encountered shortages of certain stock. The businesswoman stuck out her claw, shook the demon lord's hand, was glad to engage in honest business with him, and our hero led him out of the door.

The demon lord immediately set his followers to protest the casino and its evils. They were zealous in doing so. Unfortunately, this brought much attention to the casino; those who were reluctant to make the trip were made curious by the conflict, visited, and were decent enough judges to see that the casino's wealth was merited, and thus added to the casino's patrons.

68

The demon lord was in disbelief that, no matter what method he tried to buy the casino or take back his castle, he was repulsed by the mere fact that our heroes had complete ownership of their assets and their actions and were satisfied – largely – with minding their own business, and by minding their own business acquired vast amounts of power, though this power largely pertained to their own business. This befuddled him completely.

When he was younger, he repelled every attempt by adventurers to defeat him. His very first adventurer arrived in his throne room with a holy sword; he used that very same sword to slay him.

A party of adventurers had tried to trap him in a cursed artifact. As the artifact could not be destroyed, he was eventually set free yet not before centuries of malicious influence.

The last party of adventurers united the armies of the world in an attempt to defeat him. Their healer had let down an immense column of light; he felt every particle of his burned; and yet he lived, and crushed them all the same.

Now they were defeating him *by their own rules*. They weren't being very subtle about it either.

This track of thought gave him the idea of using their rules against them. He would acquire a great number of shares in the casino and sway the casino's decision-making.

He tried to acquire shares through the dragon-princess, yet

felt that no creature in the world could endure just her foreplay.

He attempted to possess the soldier, but the god of flatulence expelled his spirit out.

He found our hero contemptible. The businesswoman was protected by the strongest of magic: an all-star legal team.

He approached the mage at night, who was preparing the baby's room meticulously. He thought it prudent to steal on a mother-to-be in the dark; this was not true; the mage had learned a great deal through necromancy; their duel destroyed much of the castle. From his many magical attempts to seize the casino, the demon lord lacked the strength to overwhelm the mage completely; he instead, through a clever gambit, entered the unborn child. The mage then went into labor.

The mage took her son to the next shareholder's meeting and explained the predicament. She surmised the demon lord waited to assassinate her for her share in the casino, yet, having never been a child himself, did not realize that human children were fairly useless. Alas, as she had forsaken necromancy, she was unable to rend his soul out.

The shareholders understood. The mage excused herself to the women's room. The dragon-princess took the demon lord's milk bottle, discarded the milk, and replaced it with her fluids. The mage returned and fed the fussy child from the milk bottle.

The demon lord was then placed into a crib, whose wooden bars were like a prison. He found the rotation of the mobile intolerable, he found the simple and repetitive song insufferable, and he felt his diaper full. Worse, the

businesswoman removed his diaper, added her own feces
into it, and returned it back to him, before wondering aloud
how to best take the farm while its proprietor was away. He
found the experience so horrifying that he willed himself to
walk; he moved his arms, then his legs, then together in
concert; he tried to squeeze through the bars of the crib, but
his heavy diaper could not fit through; he finally recovered
enough manual dexterity to pinch the diaper's straps and
remove it, exposing his feces-crusted bottom to the air. With
this, the demon lord was now free to descend, into the casino.

69

The demon lord entered the open area of the casino. As human children were great consumers, he sought something to drink. He asked the bartender for milk; the bartender stated the bar did not serve milk; he was instead served scotch, which he greatly enjoyed.

The demon lord was then picked up by a woman, who towered over him, and allowed him to play roulette. He chose colors and numbers as he rested on her ample bosom. He frequently won, the woman holding onto the money for his general education.

The woman took the demon lord to a magic show. He found none of the tricks were impressive, as he himself was able to transplace bunnies, levitate, and cut himself in half, though he thought it was adorable for a human to do so.

The woman then took the demon lord to bet on heroes. He had never been so excited to see such inferior creatures cross a finish line, when he could have done so himself in the snap of his fingers.

After dining, the woman sought to tan on the beach. The warmth of the sun's rays, the periodical ebb and flow of the waves, and the softness of the sand almost lulled the demon lord to sleep; however, he retained control of his senses, and crawled to the outskirts of the casino, where the underpaid workers lived in shacks.

Some of them were doing troll hair. They were gracious enough to allow the demon lord to join them. Troll hair is best taken rectally. They wiped the demon lord's buttocks, which they normally loathed to do for one another, and inserted the dose. The demon lord felt every kind of bliss; he tasted colors; he saw ideas; he felt sound; and when he came to, he stole their only bottle of scotch and continued crawling around.

Some men were dicing outside of the casino, hoping to reclaim some money to enter its doors again. The demon lord was attracted to this; he won; when the loser could not repay him, he plunged a knife into his chest, covering his face with the blood of his victim.

In his soft head, the demon lord loved the casino, all enmity towards it leaving his spirit. And when he realized he was so satisfied, he immediately censured himself, and swore to murder the mage and then the rest of the casino's board members.

The bodyguards let him in, as it was not often they saw babies carry knives. He ascended the stairs, towards the boardroom, where the mage was resting after the physical exhaustion of giving birth.

As he walked very slowly, the businesswoman saw him, kicked away the knife, set him in a rocker, and rocked him until he vomited over himself and cried. She then set a bird on his head, who subsequently relieved itself on him before flying away.

Our hero and the doe passed him, the baby dragon on her back. The doe mentioned aloud how the board members could not own the haunted house, only she could, in a bid by the folk of the desert to reduce the casino's influence. She disliked owning property like the haunted house, if only because of the negative attention it brought to her name. Our hero and the doe embraced, then departed.

As the doe took pity on the demon lord and cleaned him with her tongue, an idea hatched in his mind.

70

Our heroes were alerted to the unsettling fact that the demon lord had returned to his original body and took the doe to his office to negotiate a deal over his castle. As the doe was the technical owner of the castle, there were no legal methods to prevent him from doing this. They thus armed themselves and entered the castle, whose inhabitants were defiant with the knowledge of its impending takeover.

The dwarves built them arms. The dwarves built the soldier chainmail made of mythril; for the mage they crafted a staff of gold with a sapphire catalyst; for the businesswoman they endowed her with armor reserved for the fiercest of dragons and the greatest of mounts belonging only to the greatest of kings; they were unsure what to bestow our hero, they simply made sure he could stand a knocking or two.

Each of them made their amends in case they would not survive. The soldier kissed the princess, his husband, goodbye. The mage held her son, hoping it would not be her last. The businesswoman ensured her father was well provided for. Our hero visited the grandmother, who supported him regardless of what he had done, unburdening himself.

He told her that Yusuke Kyusuke was born into another world. He immediately impressed the princess, Yuri Paizuri, with his strength, smarts, and looks, and they adventured to defeat the Dark Lord and his seven Demon Generals. Along the way they befriend the dwarf warrior Shoto Oshoto, the elf paladin Yoko Kyoko, and the warg with a heart of gold Hairi

Kairi, who were all women, who each found Yusuke attractive, and who each had large breasts. They journey through dungeons, valleys, and hot springs, and at the end of the series Yuri is possessed by the Dark Lord and becomes his fated eighth Demon General. However, the memories of their adventurers and the power of friendship ensured she has no sexual intercourse with other men even though she would spend much of her time gyrating when she was not taunting the heroes. After she is freed by the Waterfall of Purity, they defeat the Dark Lord, and Yusuke and Yuri marry, and there does not need to be any resolution for any other character. Our hero wrote all of this down and had most of the illustrations done, the draft was hidden beneath a drawer of clothes in the healer's house, and should he not make it out of this current ordeal alive the grandmother must find another illustrator to finish the light novel and publish the final edition. The grandmother nodded.

Our heroes arrived at the demon lord's castle, its path lined with crooked, barren trees. A Cerberus protected the entrance to the castle. It bit at the soldier; its teeth could not penetrate through the mail of mythril; the soldier cut the beast with his holy sword; the Cerberus farted, and each head blamed the other for passing truly noxious wind; they could not agree that whoever smelt it, dealt it; and thus they split amiably from the body they were coinhabiting. Our heroes advanced.

No sooner did they take a step into the castle they were surrounded by an ominous haze, and the cackle of three women; the women manifested themselves, revealed as the brides of the demon lord, given eternal life and invested a portion of his awesome powers.

As the brides made to do battle with their formidable

hypnotic powers, they were stopped by none other than the sisters, who challenged them to a game of basketball.

Unfortunately, having become more human than beast, the sisters were slower, weaker and shorter, and they were concerned they would break their nails. They had to make the most of their cunning, which they used to open a ten-point deficit. The sisters and the brides became sweaty; their breasts and thighs glistened with moisture; their hips and busts rubbed one another's as they tried to make plays in the court; finally they embraced and began kissing the other passionately; the sisters decided then to settle down with the demon lord's brides after consummating their whirlwind romance. Our heroes waded through their liquids, into the castle.

71

As our heroes progressed down the hallway, however, they felt it became longer and longer, and they felt the ceiling became higher and higher, then they finally fell from exhaustion. Around them they perceived a green cloud, one which they had been unable to see or smell before, and slowly they lost the use of their limbs, and their eyes became stalks. From the cloud a witch emerged, the same who had cursed the manpig with his deformity. She laughed and explained she turned them into slugs; the demon lord would reward her richly for it. She picked up our hero, whom the demon lord detested, and cursed him with the fate of a fly, buzzing around forever, never content with his existence.

This same fly flew into her mouth.

This was unfortunate as she was a hypochondriac.

She coughed, hacked, and attempted to induce vomiting to get our hero out. From desperation she picked up the businesswoman and transformed her into a toad, and swallowed said toad to swallow said fly.

Now her stomach had a fly, a toad, a snake, and a hawk in it. She consulted her doctor who recommended surgery. The surgeon removed the fly, toad, snake and hawk; when she awoke she rejoiced. Our hero, the fly, awoke on the surgeon's tray and, confused as to where he was and his present existence, flew back into the witch's mouth.

When the surgeon refused to do surgery again, as she required time to recover, she stormed from the doctor's office, bought fly pesticide and drank it in great quantities with her tea.

Now the witch was sick and remained in bed. Her niece, whom she hated, tended her. She felt she was on the verge of death, though she was pleased the damned fly was now dead. It was to her disappointment that she heard buzzing from her stomach in her dreams.

She banished the niece by throwing a teapot at her head and resolved to defeat this fly, our hero, directly. She ate copious amounts of butter and flour in the hopes of choking our hero. Unbeknownst to her, our hero needed a little snack. For her pains, she became very fat.

She ate copious amounts of beans hoping that the winds would blow our hero out. She instead earned diarrhea.

She then abstained from food, in hopes of pushing our hero through her fleshless body. Unfortunately, most diet plans do not work.

In her impulses she took a fishing hook and sunk it into her stomach, and searched for our hero in her body. She found instead her kidneys, her lungs, then her heart. Then she died.

Our heroes were returned to their original form and befriended the niece, who merely tended to her aunt to learn her magical secrets. The niece revealed the main path through the castle bore many traps; the witch was the first. With her help our heroes were led through an alternate passageway through the castle.

72

The niece led our heroes into a dark passageway that winded within the castle's walls. Unfortunately, she was not who she appeared to be; she pushed a conspicuous switch, operating a mechanism that opened the floor beneath our heroes. She laughed and leapt on her flying broomstick, only for the businesswoman, who was a dragon, to reach out her long arms and drag her down with them.

They found themselves in the demon lord's dungeons, where the blood and filth from the torture of prisoners stained the walls. Nearby they heard a groan; strapped by leather belts onto a wooden table, a golem of varied flesh freed himself and towered over our heroes, even the businesswoman. The niece explained that the demon lord had attempted to create a new human from the remains of others.

Seeing as this new man was not, by nature, violent, our heroes sought to give meaning to his life, lest he find meaning in harming them. The soldier asserted meaning came from loving one's country and giving one's life to it. The new man grasped that countries and their histories were ever-changing concepts and that loyalty is an absurd thing for a sovereign to ask for when circumstances always change. The soldier was offended.

The mage asserted meaning came from a well-educated life and that mastery of an art was the key to happiness. The new man grasped that to confuse the perfection of a skill to the perfection of a life is nonsensical, and that no amount of knowledge can prevent death and suffering; only fools believed so. The mage was offended.

The businesswoman asserted meaning came from acquiring wealth, and that she had a very lucrative position open for a shelf stocker at the casino. The new man found this somewhat agreeable as he was lazy, yet he also felt that to simply survive until death was contradictory to the idea of living, and that the tides of fortune and misfortune made any worshipping of wealth foolish; better to worship fortune instead. The businesswoman was offended only because that ploy usually worked.

The niece asserted that there was no meaning and that the demon lord created him to slaughter our heroes. The new man found this more agreeable as he found these discussions annoying.

Our hero asserted that meaning came from reading light novels, and showed him illustrations of his. The soldier, the mage, the businesswoman and the niece were appalled, would have thought light novels were pornography if the women were normally proportioned, and were concerned for the mental health of our hero and themselves, but the new man found thinking on the art, or rather, not thinking on it, so relaxing that he took our hero's argument and joined him to learn how to become an illustrator.

Our heroes felt an intense heat coming from one of the rooms within the dungeon. Entering it, they found great streams of lava coursing through it. Two elders, bone-thin, their eyes bursting from their sockets, were tending them. They were the deceased sauna proprietors, who were given a chance of vengeance against our heroes.

These were not the only persons given an opportunity for revenge. Looming in the distance was a great decaying dragon, its ribs broken open like a flower.

She breathed fire, which urged out of her stomach in a great fan; behind them, the floor beneath our heroes crumbled. They were stuck between the great flames forward or the great flames below. The mage casted various spells, attempting to reduce the dragon's fire with a blizzard; yet dragons are born considerable foes.

Our hero, not long ago, would have cowered and waited for fate to take over. But now he was an editor. He ordered his intern to dive into the fire and close the dragon's ribs. This he did; the fire erupted from her mouth, pouring into the ceiling, which caused a collapse. In the chaos our heroes fled, leaving the dragon and the sauna proprietors behind.

73

Our hero gave the new man much advice, which generally was of the theme that the new man never worked half as well or half as hard as he needed to, that our hero was able to do everything much more easily, and that he was lucky to be our hero's ward. Furthermore, he chastised the new man for having a pronounced body odor, and that he had no chance to leave his mother's basement. This was the same advice given to our hero while he worked as a light novelist. The new man apologized, and spent more time agonizing over his illustrations, which was the desired effect our hero intended, as this was the same effect it had produced in him. Our heroes continued on.

The next room emanated in a green glow; in the center was a gelatinous mound. The mound lurched toward our heroes; they cut it; it split into two slime creatures.

Our heroes did not find the slimes particularly difficult to defeat, even our hero was able to incapacitate them, yet they continued multiplying after defeat. Soon they were overwhelmed; they consumed our heroes and stole their physical attributes and memories, effectively becoming them. The slime heroes returned to the demon lord to report this success.

The demon lord was pleased and regaled them with praise; he would reward them richly, once the doe made her way into his office after many failed attempts to navigate through his labyrinthine home; they realized how much they disliked the demon lord, not as a result of possessing our heroes' personalities, merely because they felt the demon lord was a jerk. They dueled him. The resulting battle caused much commotion; the doe, believing now was an inconvenient time to speak with the demon lord, left; the demon lord, after an exhausting battle, attempted to call her back, to no avail; he had to try again the next day. In this duration, our heroes awoke, beholding before them a room full of slime children.

The businesswoman, realizing that philosophical concepts of identity were not explicable in property law, wished to slay their clones in the fear they would one day take their business; the mage, in her recent induction into motherhood, had repented of their earlier child-slaying escapades, and refused. Staff and talons were drawn, until our hero suggested a compromise: they would raise the children into an occupation that would dull their minds and cripple their sense of their rights and their ability to hold other jobs. Thus the children too would be raised as light novelists.

Our hero taught his students in the ways of an illustrator; the students were astounded by his wealth in knowledge; the other heroes were proud that there was a world in which our hero was skilled; the businesswoman was pleased by the price of their tuition and the interest rate on their loans. Very soon the artists were drawing one-shots; then serials; then publishing their own magazines; then starting their own animator studio. They were so successful that our hero felt some desire to sabotage them.

The artists adapted fables of the land into stories, as the son of the forest god overcoming twelve trials, the spriggan being swallowed by the great frog, and the dethronement of the king lion. The artists produced frames, and hired approximately twelve million light elementals to project for a large audience. Light elementals are cheap to employ as they were paid lightly, that and they were non-union. They showed the films to an audience, who loved them. The artists developed theme parks after their films, which attracted great crowds.

Now the businesswoman was concerned. The artists were so successful that fewer people went to the casino. She was more convinced than ever to slay the slime artists. Our hero, who was not given credit by the artists, agreed. The mage, however, resisted. Though the bodies of the slime were adult, they were technically born yesterday, and thus still children.

As business-minded folk often think in terms of competition, the businesswoman commissioned our hero to create a film of his own. Our hero was excited to make something of himself and earn praises above his students. He went quickly to work, and worked hard; the film was published right away.

The film was inscrutable, and because it was inscrutable, critics saw it as obscene; some saw it as immoral; some saw its creator as disturbed; others stressed it could not be shown to children; they generally agreed it was stupid; most thought it was boring; everyone thought it should be burned; it drove some light elementals to their self-destruction.

The businesswoman seized the chance to argue that all films were unnecessary, and petitioned for a censorship arm of the city's parliament; the creation of this group was approved, and they proved so competent at this sole task that no film passed their scrutiny. Thus the artists were now unemployed, though the mage was very happy to fill out more rooms in her castle.

74

The new man alone remained of our hero's disciples as he felt art was not meant for mass consumption, but for the contemplation of the happy few. Our hero rolled his eyes. His pupil was a thinker.

Our heroes, and the niece, caught up with the former sauna proprietors, who quickly petitioned for a truce. As our heroes were tired and dirty from their encounter with the slime, they ought to relax and clean themselves in a spa. Our heroes, who were indeed tired and dirty, agreed.

Our heroes entered the sauna. As the soldier was married, the niece underaged, the mage a widow, the businesswoman a dragon, and the new man hardly a person, they did not split off into gendered saunas; in fact, after enduring countless of adventures of horrors they did not have much of a sexual appetite left. They relaxed in the other's presence and chatted blandly.

Unfortunately, the waters beneath them churned; as it turned out, the sauna was a water elemental, and it drained them into the castle's moat, which was filled with blood. Crocodiles and alligators, who did not discriminate toward the other, swarmed around them, and would have eaten them if they had not been long dissatisfied with their living conditions, particularly that they lived in blood, and not saltwater. They aided our heroes back into the dungeon to retrieve their belongings; the water elemental, who was really a blood elemental, was tamed by the mage, who was familiar with crimson waves; and the crocodiles and alligators made stew of the sauna proprietors, as there were very few sources of meat which lived in a river of blood.

In the following room they encountered the werewolf, who had never forgiven our hero for what he had done to his beloved forest. He bit our heroes in turn, and they all became helpless dogs. They played, sniffed the other's rears, and whined constantly. The werewolf felt bad for our heroes, who had never been dogs before and so succumbed to natural habits, and vowed to raise them as his own litter. He saw his pack go through dog elementary school; gave them dog supplies; packed their dog lunches; wiped their dog noses; saw them through dog college; helped them through hard dog financial times; and then embraced their dog children, his grandchildren. Now revenge meant little to him, and his heart softened considerably in old age.

Unfortunately our hero had been a werewolf before, and in the relaxation of security he bit deeply into the werewolf's jugular veins; blood splashed onto the dungeon wall, the dungeon floor, the dungeon ceiling, themselves becoming werewolves; the werewolf tried to breathe, and staggered; he searched for needles, they were in silver; he searched for bandages, he only found them in silver; he sought witch's hazel, it was wolfsbane; he cursed his ignorance in botany, and died; our heroes returned to their regular forms, and gave the mysterious dogs to their unemployed artists to tend.

75

Guarding the dungeon to the castle's main floor were a horde of undead. Though the soldier's holy sword was powerful indeed, they understood they would not be strong enough to defeat the demon lord without most of their strength. Instead, they pretended to be undead: they thought older forms of music were better, they thought they were wise in politics without having held any office or participated in any public discussions, they ignored traffic lights and checked their phones on crowded staircases, and gave unwanted advice. The undead determined they were mindless too, and they made their way up.

Contrary to the niece's warnings, the main floor was empty; they roamed through room after room of antique books, furniture and other curios. They wished to retaliate against the niece, but they found her to be in earnest.

They entered a large banquet hall, whose table was furnished with a sumptuous feast; the dishes consisted of fattened griffon liver, manticore flank steaks, sea serpent pie, and chilled mandragora. Feeling famished, they sat to dine; the mage ate the mandragora, the soldier bit into the steak, the businesswoman had some pie, and our hero had an omelet.

Our hero clung to his sides, as he felt great pain inside of him. From his bowels he heard a voice: "You had long forgotten me, imprisoned in that cage, but now I am released, and will revenge myself on you." It was the necromancer, whose spells the mage had stolen, and whom our hero had abandoned in the egg.

Our heroes were uncertain of what to do. As he possessed only our hero's stomach, it did not seem there was much he could do. Our hero then consumed large amounts of food; it came out through the other end; the dung was animated; the necromancer had created mud pie golems.

Our heroes would have done battle with the golems, had the new man not stopped them, as he felt compassion for those who were given life unnaturally and not by their own will, as had happened to him. He persuaded them to no longer do the necromancer's doing. They relented, and became artists.

Unfortunately, they were very bad at creating art. Their art, in the new man's mind, was lowbrow, childish, and full of cheap toilet humor. The other heroes were not impressed either, but the new man was particularly offended. Worse, the mud pies' works were very popular and drew a large crowd.

The new man petitioned the censorship arm of parliament to ban their books. Though parliament found the works crude, they did not see their works as having a particularly morally-debilitating effect.

As the new man fought his own battles, no one had noticed our hero swallowing an unusual number of chickens, turkeys and geese whole, bones and all. Bone after bone fell through his rear; when enough had fallen out, they assembled into a bone golem. This bone golem too was incensed by the mud pies' "art", and created his own works; however, they were hollow and spineless. Worse, because they were supposed to have high-minded ideals and preached often to their audience, they were confused with the new man's works, and

the new man and the bone golem had their authorships
confused.

The new man realized then that all lives were not sacred
and slew his fellow creatures, mud pies and bone golems
both. He then took their combined works, set our hero onto a
chair, and read them all to him, which effect resembled a
laxative. The necromancer's spirit left our hero's body; he
repented of his crimes against humanity, as he did not realize
that the worst crime against humanity is to make bad art, and
the second worst crime is to give birth to those who make bad
art. For his late redemption he went to heaven, where he
struck a match with the saint, both of them being shy loners.

76

The forks, plates, trays and candlesticks of the dining table shook; they were made out of gold, and they were possessed by the golden elementals our hero and the businesswoman had slain. They sought vengeance. They combined into a great idol, towering over the castle, and revealed that, because of our heroes' actions, great worship was given to a new god, a god of gold. This same god destroyed the casino, ruined their best necklaces and earrings and depleted their bank accounts. Our heroes were now paupers. The demon lord rejoiced.

Our heroes convinced the city to base their currency on corn. Our heroes were able to resume the productivity of their businesses quickly, and created in the process a god of corn, who fought the god of gold.

Furthermore, they advocated for protections against loss, particularly from gods of gold, such as a centralized bank, disaster relief, and universal income. Therefore no one associated wealth strictly with gold or corn, and once the god of corn overthrew the god of gold, the god of corn itself fell, both on the demon lord, who then had to reschedule his appointment with the doe.

Around our heroes the food of the great banquet perished; our heroes were forced to pinch their noses; a great stench overcame the castle. Descending to them was the saint of gas, propelled by the great gust emitted from his rear end. He argued passionately that the god of gas damned our heroes and, as his emissary, it was his duty to slay all heathens.

With a single shout, the saint of gas caused them to flatulate violently, such that they released other things through their rears. Our heroes scattered, searching for the restroom. There was only one issue: the saint had removed all the toilet paper from the stalls.

Our heroes fled to the casino, which had been quickly rebuilt after the god of gold's destruction, albeit, instead of gold chandeliers and fountains, these were made of corn, and sought to replace their undergarments. Yet, as they donned a fresh set of apparel, the saint of gas shouted again, causing them to release wind more intensely than before; the wind was so strong, it blew a hole through their undergarments; the wind was so strong it knocked them on the floor; the wind was so strong it blew them from their offices to the main floor of the casino. Here, battered and bloody, the casino patrons and their employees laughed at them for their misfortunes. Our heroes faced their greatest enemy yet.

Because of the energy required to summon such winds, our heroes were in desperate need to eat; however, the saint diffused his stench through the entire casino, thus causing them to retch any food or drink they attempted to consume. They attempted to isolate themselves from the rest of the casino by retreating to the elevator, but the saint let out the most rancid gas yet inside. The mage cried, the businesswoman fainted, and the soldier was near tearing his nostrils out. Our hero tried to aid them, but the saint shouted once more, causing our hero to break wind so intensely he smashed a table into pieces.

Dizzy and exhausted, our heroes could only observe as they felt the ground of the casino shake beneath them. Our hero looked out at the window; the saint had erected an immense balloon over the casino, and released enormous winds from his mouth to lift the casino aloft. He intended to raise the casino many yards off the air and dash it to the grounds, to punish the sinners.

Our heroes consulted the soldier; the soldier observed the holy sword had not lost strength, in spite of the saint's accusations. Our heroes deliberated, and the soldier concluded that he must make the ultimate sacrifice. He took the sword, placed it within himself, becoming a saint of gas.

The soldier ascended to the heavens, dark with the noxious winds, and confronted the saint of gas. He argued strenuously with the saint, causing a schism in this very new religion. Each of them wrote religious tracts; they argued over scripture and canon; finally they petitioned to their god; their god told them to stand on a mountain; a great and powerful wind tore the mountains apart and shattered the rocks, but their god was not in the wind. A voice asked them who produced the wind; the saint said it was the god of gas; but the soldier proclaimed, "Whoever smelt it, dealt it."

The saint then experienced intense abdominal pains, and flatulated every atom of his existence out, for his impiety. Our heroes took a much-needed rest before continuing onward in their quest.

77

The battle of the gods destroyed the main staircase. Our heroes were forced to advance through the castle by a side staircase, leading to the exterior of the castle. Outside they saw a wide, vast night sky and its stars burning bright, providing light for their heroic endeavors.

In the distance they could see a black object obscuring the moon; it grew larger; it loomed towards them; they fled up the staircase, to the top of the keep; the undead dragon opened her jaws and breathed great floods of flame, bathing the castle in fire. She flew away shrinking into the eye of the moon. Our heroes were now trapped.

The dragon swooped down again, blanketing the keep with fire. The water elemental, which the mage had tamed, shielded our heroes, though a great deal of her body was destroyed. The dragon landed, and with her immense strength rend the rock of the tower's masonry. The businesswoman lunged at her with talons and teeth; however, as the businesswoman was not a true dragon, she was repulsed easily.

The businesswoman intended only to serve as a distraction so the mage could finish the preparations for her magic circle. Ice trapped the dragon's limbs; she was unable to move.

The soldier raised his sword and attempted to strike the dragon, yet one breath of hers set the holy sword ablaze and blew him away. The mage tried to pierce her skull with lightning, yet one mighty flick of her tail knocked her staff, the sole catalyst of her awesome powers, away. Our hero, however, had one magic of his own to rely on.

The dragon melted the ice shackling her, and thundered her anger to the dark heavens. However, below her, our hero presented the one thing that made her anger pause: her son.

She quietened, then touched nostrils with the boy. Her anger subsided.

The moon was obscured again; swooping down, it was a different black figure; the pope of the forest, the father of the son, arrived, with various states of emotion, first wanting to avenge himself on our heroes, then wanting to destroy the child that caused him pain, then wanting to destroy the mother for having the child originally.

The dragons dueled through their breaths; however, having become one with the divine tree, the pope's breath grew foliage, whose nature was of fire and could not be burned down. The mother was overwhelmed; a tree pierced through her, like a lance.

The pope dove in to take his revenge, only for our hero to pick the son up and lift his tail to show his rear. Unable to resist the bottoms of boys, the pope redirected his attention, allowing the soldier to stick the holy sword into his rear. The pope, befitting his age, let out a millennium of gas that he had to withhold from the congregation, and was propelled far out of the recesses of the world; he drifted in the expanse of space, with no wind under his wings to fly; trapped and powerless, he was perpetually horrified by his predicament; eventually, he stopped thinking.

Fortunately, the mother dragon was undead, and able to remove the tree lance. She had no enmity against our heroes now, however, she wished herself to raise her son, as she could not trust our hero based on his actions.

As the mage had forsaken necromancy, it was difficult to give the mother a flesh-and-blood body. The mage then brought her team of unemployed artists, who used every technique of CGI to make the dragon look living and used special effects to make her feel warm and produce milk, as would be needed for her son. People mistook movie magic for reality and readily accepted the dragon's transformation. Our hero did not think the doe would like this development; they would discuss custody of the child later.

78

Our heroes descended from the top of the keep, winding their way towards the demon lord's throne room. They entered a long hall lined with decorated columns. A thick fog filled the room; from the fog a great warrior formed, a head taller than our heroes, wielding an immense axe.

The soldier dueled the warrior; the warrior demonstrated considerable strength and skill, which traits were not required of soldiers, and defeated him; rather than turn against the remaining heroes, he desired to duel our hero, for he sensed heroic blood in him.

Our hero agreed; the two faced one another; our hero excused himself and went to the bathroom. The warrior acquiesced; our hero departed; he found no exits in the bathroom; much time went by. The warrior asked if our hero needed anything; our hero responded that there was no toilet paper; the warrior, being of the spirit realm, where there are no physical limitations, produced toilet paper, and assured our hero he could produce anything our hero required, as hand soap, tampons, scented candles.

Much time passed. Finally our hero left the bathroom. The warrior picked up his weapon; however, our hero recommended, for the fairness of the duel, that the warrior relieve himself in the bathroom too. The warrior felt he needed to refreshen his ectoplasm. As soon as the door shut, our heroes ran.

Within this long hallway they encountered a goblin with decorated armor and a shining sword. He was the hero of the goblin people and found the demon lord preferable to our heroes, who were the cause, direct or indirect, of the deaths of many tribes. Our hero offered himself up for a duel and the goblin a chance to use the restroom. The goblin agreed as the journey was long and the sight of the water elemental inspired flow. He was slain by the warrior in the bathroom, as the bathroom allowed only one occupant, and the warrior was having some trouble passing ectoplasm.

Our heroes encountered a golem, ingeniously made by the dwarves centuries ago to defend an ancient kingdom. Our hero meant to duel it; he recommended it oil its joints; the golem was defeated by the warrior, who tried to wash his hands, though he had none.

Our heroes encountered one of the demon lord's generals, who was a master swordsman; our hero recommended he freshen himself in the bathroom; the swordsman had no concept of hygiene; our hero recommended he relieve himself; the swordsman had taught himself to discipline his bowels for a thousand years; our hero recommended checking himself in the mirror, as he perceived a bit of spinach in his teeth; he assented, and lost to the warrior, who was checking his hair in the mirror.

The warrior, now prepared, was able to start the duel proper. He and our hero faced one another; our hero slightly relieved himself there, after a day of sitting on the toilet. He pleaded for the warrior to stop; it was clear that the warrior had an advantage.

Our hero argued that he knew nothing concerning swords; the warrior threw his axe aside and raised his fists. Our hero argued he had bad eyesight; the warrior occluded his. Our hero argued he did not get much sleep last night; the warrior spent the night on a lumpy bed.

Finally, they agreed on an honorable duel that used our hero's best strength, consisting of picking up balls and placing them in a bucket, with a particular wide part of their bodies. The game was set; our hero squatted; he clenched, as he had in his drug-trafficking days; one ball fell into the bucket.

The warrior squatted; he clenched; he grasped onto the object, which was a totem capable of trapping spirits; thus his buttocks, then his body, then his head was absorbed into the totem.

79

Rinsed of all malice, the warrior in the totem spoke: he wished to aid our heroes, for he had once been an adventurer whose heart was set on defeating the demon lord.

Many years ago he, a wizard, a healer, a thief and a bard roamed the new world, slaying monsters, aiding cities in need, and discovering magical creatures, all towards the purpose of defeating the demon lords. They and their allies had cornered the demon lords in one part of the world and had come close to defeating them, only to succumb to their wiles. Now he had spent many years trapped in this demon lord's castle, protecting his cursed treasure, a mockery of his living self.

When he discovered that the demon lord had no treasure remaining to protect, he was pleasantly surprised. When he discovered that our heroes were unwilling to give up the rights to the castle, he was very confused, but nonetheless still eager to help them.

In the long hallway, our heroes encountered the pirates of the giant's stomach. They had gotten bored of peaceful living, and were promised limitless plundering by the demon lord, should they defeat our heroes. Our heroes scoffed, as they presented a very small threat; the pirates called them sissies and land lubbers, which insults incensed them.

The pirates proposed a duel in dice; the businesswoman defeated them; they proposed a knife game; the businesswoman defeated them; they proposed drinking; the businesswoman, who had the stomach of a dragon, defeated them; she defeated them in Russian Roulette too.

Out of money, out of men, and out of pride, the captain of the pirates wore the amulet as the demon lord had instructed. This was the same amulet the mage's mentor was trapped in. The archmage dueled our mage, with great tongues of flame, great baleful winds, and great bolts of lightning.

The archmage, who had always thought little of his pupil, did not believe a woman could equal him in sorcery. The university the archmage had been a professor of and the mage had graduated from took notice of this, and agreed it amounted to discrimination; they forced the archmage to resign. Though the archmage always thought little of the university and did not mind leaving, he was particularly unhappy that he had to resign in such a disgraceful way, arguing that it amounted to discrimination against himself. This lapse in judgment allowed the mage to gain the upper hand.

As a last resort, the archmage summoned the spirit of the minotaur, the mage's on-off lover and husband, threatening to destroy his soul forever, removing him from the cycle of life and rebirth. The mage was agonized by this threat, and the archmage soundly defeated her.

The warrior, his noble soul angered by such cheap tricks, thereupon possessed our hero, whom he shared heroic blood with, and took up his axe. However, our hero's muscular strength was far lacking compared to his own, and he missed his mark, which was the archmage's head; instead, the head of the axe cut the archmage's belt, which effect lowered his trousers, revealing his micropenis. Though this was really the pirate's micropenis, rumor spread very quickly; universities across the world were disgusted; college coeds laughed at him; ashamed, the archmage fled back into the amulet, which the mage desired to destroy. Instead, in her final act of necromancy, she sealed the soul of the pirate in the amulet as well, so that the archmage would spend eternity with someone whom he regarded as his complete inferior; and the other, his.

80

As the end of the long hall stood the dryad. Our heroes assumed she too longed for vengeance; she assured them she wanted nothing so petty; she merely informed them that the god of the forest had himself a father, who was the demon lord.

A spectral white buck manifested before them; it shrieked, summoning many lamps, made out of the hides of his slain descendants, enrobing himself with them. Though the buck was empowered by the anger of so many spirits, he was still newly created, and thus the mage prepared to set him aflame.

However, the buck fused two relics together, reanimating the body of our hero's son by the doe, and this broke his heart. Though our hero did not see himself as a father, he saw the boy indisputably as his son. Our hero's willingness to fight was our heroes' as well, and so the wraith defeated them.

The wraith, flushed with satisfaction concerning his victory, sought to destroy the casino as well. He saw many of his descendants transfixed by the slots; many operated the brothels around the casino; most of them were drinking their sorrows away; worst, he could hardly recognize them. Some were hirsute, some were very tall, some were very narrow, some had long hair, some had terrible body odor, some had prominent brow ridges, some had poor posture, some had stubby tails, and yet all were mostly, and disappointingly, smooth skinned, upright, self-restrained and anxious humans.

The wraith chastised his descendants for their addiction to gambling; the wraith chastised his descendants for selling their bodies; the wraith chastised his descendants for wasting their lives away. They were supposed to gambol and frolic through the woods without clothing, sleeping under the sun, eating what come may, obeying only their feral selves. They responded all that wraiths had no say on what the people of the present are doing and enduring. The wraith was furious, and argued that he had spent so much time and energy fostering their generations. They each gave him the bird, which was a gesture not known in his life, yet he was offended nevertheless.

He prepared to whip a great wind to raze the casino, only to be stopped by a greater force. As a result of their present circumstances, the former forest creatures had forgotten large passages of their past, yet, out of some innate drive to recall their origin, constructed a new source for their tree of life. They thus believed in a new god of the forest, very different from the actual god of the forest, and this god defended the casino. The wraith could not believe his eyes, and beheld this new god.

This new god resembled an ape, for this creature most resembled the humans; this god was not very bright, and relied on brute strength; it had no sense of dignity; it frequently defecated, and often into its hands; it then threw the results at other people. The god was a perfect summation of how the former forest creatures believed their prior existence had been: simple, happy, but crude, ugly, and unintelligent.

This affected the wraith greatly, as he understood the new

god was a caricature of him, and he did not perceive himself as ugly and stupid. He possessed the golden goose, which had been given to our heroes from the giantess, and amassed a large fortune by laying eggs. He sought to use this wealth to sway the former forest folk, his descendants, that he, in fact, was intelligent and handsome, and that life had been better, and life could be better with a simple and painless reversion to their simpler ways, through a battery of advertisements and podcasts.

Though these tactics were able to persuade a few of the forest folk, particularly those who had been worms and bats in the previous life, many of the others were puzzled by the perks of being an animal. The forest god argued: he enjoyed being nude; they felt he didn't have much to show. He enjoyed frolicking; they thought it was a waste of a life. He had enjoyed endless copulation; as it turned out, only *he* could enjoy this. Finally, he thought being an animal was more honest and decent than being a human; but he had been the strongest in a world defined by strongest-of-the-fittest, and so it was not difficult to believe that he thought *he* was decent.

The forest god did not relent, and in fact doubled his efforts. He gave lectures, in buildings he bought, he gave conferences, whose audiences he paid for, he ran for prime minister, to show that he, in fact, was a wise and proud person, only to understand that no one thought politicians were intelligent, particularly the person who desired to be their leader.

He drank initially to get through these speeches, and then drank voluminously to numb the pain of being rejected. There began to be great holes in his memories. It was then revealed

that, during these blackouts, he dressed and acted as a
human, and propositioned himself as a human when he
allowed himself to be mounted by horses. Out of shame, he
threw himself over a cliff, releasing the many anguished,
vengeful souls that had gathered under his power.

Our hero and his son had one last exchange. Our hero
apologized for neglecting him. His son didn't necessarily
forgive him, but he also did not condemn him, for he never
learned to speak. This gave our hero, and thus our heroes,
the strength to continue fighting.

81

Unfortunately, the dryad still had many tricks up her sleeve. She had created a great monstrosity, two hundred feet tall, composed only of razor-sharp teeth, talons and horns, to defeat our heroes. Unfortunately, this same great, massive monster perished of heart failure.

She then revealed her next masterpiece: a great monstrosity, two hundred feet tall, composed only of razor-sharp teeth, talons and horns, but it was also very cute. Our heroes were very reluctant to slay it; the cost of their reluctance was the destruction of several cities, as a result of the monster perishing from heart failure, and falling upon them. Thankfully, none of the cities did business with our heroes.

She then revealed her next masterpiece: a much smaller monstrosity, that devoured all in sight, and bred very quickly. Unfortunately she did not create a female specimen.

She then revealed her next masterpiece: a monstrosity whose death released a deadly virus. Unfortunately, our heroes had nothing against it, and the monster very much wanted to live.

The dryad revealed more and more creations, that were faster, stronger, and more resilient than the last, but the emerging theme is that they each wished to live meaningful, fulfilling lives, and the various mutations she had introduced, while increasing their lethality, decreased the length of their mortality and quality of life. She then considered whether she herself was the monster, and contented herself to live only for crossword puzzles.

It was then the new man realized that our heroes were not truly good, and, as an entity strictly created for profit, did irreparable damage to other races, the environment, and the socioeconomic welfare of the workers of the world. He protested; others joined him; they blocked the throne room, which advantaged the demon lord, whose appointment was delayed by the doe who wished to get her nails done.

Our heroes discussed. The businesswoman had a strong inclination to slay all of the protestors, as their claims were illegitimate, while the other heroes were more sympathetic. The new man, meanwhile, had developed an increasingly ironic and scathing repertoire that was very funny but ultimately had no practical effect except to draw certain bearded individuals, whose stench offended the demon lord.

They found the protestors were strangely resilient from buy-outs of their beliefs, as they themselves didn't know precisely what they believed. They attempted to deceive the protestors into transplanting, but these were people who were neither inclined to move nor lift a finger. They hired moles to sway their opinions, but the protestors regarded everyone and everything with intense sarcasm, suspicion, and eye-rolling; this was also the reason why they got nothing done.

The protestors crafted several slogans railing against the businesswoman. The businesswoman was enraged and wished to slay them all. Our hero conceived of a good compromise.

He announced that the casino would commit to protecting the environment; enforcing fair workplace rules; compensating the former forest folk, whose literal bloodline had been diluted in order for the casino to benefit by their weakness; and enshrining these commitments in gold in the casino's mezzanine. The protestors cheered and dispersed; the casino did exactly the latter of our hero's promises, and nothing more.

Only the new man remained, for he was so passionately disillusioned with all of humanity that no outcome of any substance could satisfy him, short of the total absence of humanity. Our hero spoke with him; he railed that our hero made work to entertain himself and other people, which mistake he would correct by making work that would enlighten people; he railed that our hero made fetishistic work that appealed to people's carnal desires, which mistake he would correct by inspiring the nobler side of his audience; he railed that our hero made work where the hero by needs must win, which mistake he would correct by creating work where the hero could not always win, no matter what strength or wit he possessed, and in fact the hero did not always have pure intentions. Soon he was so up his own ass that he perished from lack of oxygen, and the way to the throne room opened up.

82

Before our heroes could enter the throne room, they were delivered a message from the grandmother. They returned to her residence, where she baked our heroes cookies, boiled for them hot chocolate, and set out comfortable chairs and board games. Our heroes, who were embroiled in many battles recently, took to this comfort easily; when they made to stand up and go, the grandmother insisted they stay longer, commenting under her breath that so few people visited her in her older years. Thus they stayed.

Our heroes were now pondering whether they needed to slay the grandmother. They discussed hiding her cane, substituting her insulin, pushing her down a flight of stairs, and removing her carbon monoxide detector.

They shoved her into the oven with which she was baking pies; she seemed pleased with this as she complained of late that the thermostat was not working.

They displaced her spectacles; as a result, she delayed our heroes even further by moving twice as slowly.

They dipped her teeth in arsenic; this was nothing compared to the chemicals her doctor prescribed.

They felt there was no choice but to behead her. Then she announced a trip to the casino. Our heroes were elated, as the demon lord's castle was on the way to the casino. Unfortunately they could not name a chaperone.

The mage asked her unemployed artists; they were very busy lying in bed.

The soldier asked his husband; she was very busy with her book club.

Our heroes asked the dragon; she was catching up on lost time with her son, and wondered aloud how that time became lost.

The business's income was dear, and the businesswoman disliked expending it. They wished to remind the grandmother she had a granddaughter, but did not know if they were touching on a delicate situation.

They finally petitioned the one man who had much time on his hands: the demon lord, for the doe was now visiting a doctor for an errant cough. The demon lord agreed, not understanding the grandmother moved at a fraction of a person's speed.

The grandmother was the antithesis of evil in that she was very boring. She made safe bets, did not partake in alcohol, enjoyed bland foods, and engaged in banal conversations. She wondered if the demon lord had a girlfriend. He did not, though he did not add that he had many concubines.

The grandmother asked what the demon lord did for a living. He responded that he lived to be evil. The grandmother asked if this profession paid well. Generally, it did.

The grandmother wished to introduce him to her granddaughter. The demon lord did not want to meet her. She asked why he did not want to. He replied that this was incompatible with his profession. She wondered aloud what sort of profession disallowed a nice man to meet a nice, youngish woman as her granddaughter.

Now the demon lord sought to kill her. He felt his evil was

indisputable, and that it was ludicrous for a grandmother to challenge it. Nevertheless, he refrained from doing so, as it was not a good look for a demon lord to defeat an old woman.

He tried to hasten her by summoning demon steeds. She took longer to mount them than to walk.

He tried to hasten her by liquifying her food. She found the chicken much harder to eat, especially with a fork.

He tried to hasten her by operating the slots for her. But that defeated the purpose of her having fun.

As the demon lord sat outside the venue hall, as he did not find standup comedy very funny, and contemplated on his life, he realized that concerning himself with the optics of killing old women constituted an obedience to order and society, which was against the idea of evil. He then sought to kill the old woman.

As the comedy magician needed a volunteer, the grandmother hobbled onstage and was given a saw to cut the assistant in half. She cut, or attempted to; after many feeble attempts, the assistant split in half; this was in actuality the demon lord, and he used this incident as a pretense to punch the grandmother. He did not understand that hitting old women was close on the moral scale to killing old women.

Fortunately, this did not matter as the punch put the grandmother in a serious condition, and she was taken to the hospital. The city was incensed, and stormed the demon lord's castle. Our heroes entered the throne room.

83

Our heroes discussed with the warrior a plan to defeat the demon lord. They were able to take their time as the citizens were quarreling with the demon lord.

The dragon princess first approached the demon lord as the representative of the city. Immediately she found him quite handsome and was smitten with him. Her love, however, was more dangerous than her wrath, and in her excitement she spat a great many dragon's seed, children willing to do her bidding, which was to subdue the demon lord and make love to him. The demon lord desperately threw his own dragon's teeth, which became spartoi, and the forces of the dragon princess and the demon lord fought; the dragon's seed won, but the dragon princess had become bored, and very tired, and now understood why all of her lovers were so sleepy after coupling.

Entering the room next was the citizen's army. The demon lord prepared himself for a great battle, as he had done in the past: he had repelled countless ballistae, heat rays and golems. Instead, the army merely told the demon lord to quieten down, as was requested by the citizens. The demon lord agreed until they relayed that he was required to attend court, to determine if he should be tried. He thought this was ridiculous. They asserted the castle was much louder than he realized. There were no good times. Finally he relented and chose a date next week. They promptly left.

Entering the room next were his fans, who were very excited to see him defeat our heroes. He would have been pleased by this too, but he, for the time being, wished to focus on actually defeating our heroes. They wished to have their faces signed. The resulting labor cramped his good hand.

Entering the throne room next was the recruiter, who sensed that many of the castle's army had been depleted by our heroes. The demon lord transformed him into a toad. Yet, even as a toad, his innate nature was to recommend people. The demon lord relented, agreeing to his services after the battle.

Entering the throne room next was the tailor, who sensed that the demon lord's attire was not fitting for a final battle. The demon lord was intrigued, though he had no gold left. He agreed to take out a loan, in exchange for more appropriate clothing.

Entering the throne room next were his mummies, who, as a result of their work as janitors, were running out of wraps. The demon lord agreed, and dismissed them. The mummies demanded action now, or they would go on strike. As the only materials left in the castle, the demon lord gave up his nice clothing.

Entering the throne room next was the grandmother's granddaughter, who simply slapped him in the face and left. The slap hurt more than any attack by any adventurer in his long lifetime.

Finally, our heroes arrived. He admitted to himself these were the strongest adventurers he had ever faced, and gave them the best speech he had ever given. He told them how countless of adventurers had faced him, only to fall. He told them how he was an inevitability, a constant truth in this world, while they were merely his audience. He told them how his reign of evil will be forever and grow even more powerful once he had his castle, their casino, and their farm.

This is what he wrote and what he imagined in his head. He was allowed to say very little of this. The mage drew a large ritual circle around the throne room; with her fellow adventurers as a catalyst, she sealed the demon lord in a bottle of ale.

84

This was not the end of the demon lord, however. The warrior had learned from past adventures that the sealed demon lord had to be disposed of.

They sought a holy place to dissipate the demon lord's evil over the course of centuries. They visited a nunnery, whose rooms and graveyard were filled with virgins, deceased and living. They spoke to the mother superior; she asserted they did not have nearly as many nuns needed; they showed her gold; she believed she miscounted; for this mother superior's love for clothing was a bad habit.

Unfortunately the demon lord's evil was so overwhelming that he transformed the nuns into succubi, who were still wearing their religious habits, which made them twice as seductive as regular succubi.

They then visited a holy see, and made the same offer to the bishop there. Unfortunately they did not understand sees are not as holy as they were conventionally thought, and the bishop became a vampire, who continued his immortality by draining the life essence of his catamites.

They then visited a dairy, as our hero misunderstood what "holy" meant. The Swiss produced was more evil than usual.

They then visited a pin, to inquire as to how many angels could dance on it. As it turned out, no angels could, and the possessed pin pricked our hero's fingers.

They then visited the desert people's man of the rocks, though the desert people nowadays believed more in the casino than their god.

They then visited the divine tree; allergy season was more intense than usual.

They then consulted the god of flatulence, who directed them to build a temple. The temple would have no entrances, except for one hole in the ceiling, which could be sealed by will with a covering twenty cubits thick. The priest or initiate would have strong men remove the covering, squat over the hole, and give earnest prayers to the temple, whose interior would be decorated with statues of the god surrounding the cursed bottle of ale.

This was a very effective means of sealing the demon lord, who did not want to leave the vessel and enter the fervent prayers of the god of flatulence's devotees. However, every brick of the temple began to smell, even the exterior, as the builders were a cubit short. The temple was then destroyed by a smoker.

Our heroes then determined to place the demon lord somewhere unfathomably far so as to diffuse his evil safely. They placed him in the deepest trench of the ocean; this produced very mean fish.

They then threw the bottle of ale into the darkness of space; they were visited by very cross extraterrestrials.

They then threw the bottle into the deepest cave; they awoke a very large lizard.

They then asked the nightmare, who remained ambivalent to the demon lord as in life, to take the bottle into dreams; this produced too many bedwetters.

They then threw the bottle down the giant's gullet, as a kind of cheat for his wife's imposed diet; the demon lord gave him very bad gas.

They then considered using the bottle's original purpose, to hold ale, as a way to make the demon lord more drunk than evil; they decided this was too blissful an eternity than he deserved.

85

Our heroes then deliberated to beat the evil out of the demon lord, and released him. Before they could duel, he asked if he could recite his speech. They declined.

The niece of the witch decided then she had taken this too far and longed to separate from the group. The demon lord acquiesced. Our heroes did not. They thought he was a sissy. Incensed, he asked to consult the dictionary on what a sissy actually was. Disturbed by the entry, he sought to fight the niece. As she was overwhelmed by his awesome power, they decided on the fair competition of baking.

The two chefs were tasked with baking the city's favorite food, pie. The niece's was delicious; the demon lord's was burnt.

The two were tasked with baking bread. The niece's was chewy and firm; the demon lord's was burnt.

The two were tasked with baking cake. The niece's was moist; the demon lord's was burnt.

The demon lord accused the judges of cheating, as his dishes tasted fine to him. Through investigation they found that all food tasted burnt to him because his head was aflame.

Nevertheless, they took the accusation seriously and made their own dishes, which were bland or bad compared to the niece's. The niece was simply exceptionally good at cooking, possibly as a result of tending to her aunt's cauldron so often; whisking butter and whipping cream required similar skills as mixing eye of newt and toe of frog. She thereon decided to become a baker over being a witch and living the perils of that latter lifestyle, not for any love of baking, but for lack of passion and being adequate at anything else.

Our heroes and the demon lord were now one-zero.

The warrior proposed to duel the demon lord, to redeem himself for his failures in the past. He possessed our hero's body once more; now more attuned to our hero's body, he was able to move more gracefully and strike more powerfully. The demon lord was more accustomed to this type of duel, and the two duelists fought admirably and beautifully.

The warrior possessed more strength; the demon lord, however, was more slippery; he disarmed the warrior, after exhausting him, and taunted him before killing him and our hero.

However, the warrior was not bested, as he knew he was inadequate now as he had been so many years ago. He was not the same man, as he was not in the same body. He passed wind, which distracted the demon lord. With a lusty shout and a powerful leap, he sat on the demon lord. The demon lord struggled; he sank lower; the demon lord struggled to breathe; he sank lower; the demon lord no longer wished to breathe; he stopped sinking.

He asked the demon lord to plead for mercy. The demon lord did not stir. The warrior passed wind. The demon lord moved a finger, tapping the warrior's leg as a signal of submission.

Yet the warrior refused the demon lord mercy, as he had denied mercy to countless others. He tightened his hold on his head; he strained every muscle; one could hear skin, blood vessels, bones being crushed; then our hero's buttocks closed upon themselves, and let out the dust of the demon lord's head; the body fell down, motionless; the evil was vanquished.

As the warrior celebrated his victory and his vengeance, an arrow was shot through his, and our hero's, heart. The demon lord's headless body stood, a bow with its arrow gone in its hands. It then took the head of the cherub statue whose bow and arrow it removed, set it aflame, and placed it where the head had been. The demon lord had revived, mortality being nothing to him.

Though the warrior's time in this world was severed, he sought to save our hero's life. He removed the arrow carefully and, using the magic inherent in heroic blood, recovered from the wound only enough to allow our hero's heart to continue.

The warrior's spirit passed onto the afterlife. In his prior life he had served his daimyo to his death; in this life he served his friends to the death; he was now ready to go unto the next, ready to brave any and all obstacles and doubts.

86

Now our heroes and the demon lord could fight. The mage threw fireballs; the demon lord swallowed them, and spit them back; the soldier swung the holy sword at him; he evaded them and gave blows of his own; the businesswoman used her claws; the demon lord used his, for he was the father of dragons; our hero watched; the demon lord emerged unscathed, for no magic or blade hitherto could defeat him.

These scenes were illustrated by our hero, to demonstrate that for our heroes fighting would be tantamount to surrender.

They instead poured living slime into our hero's rear. From the remains of the demon lord's head, the slime had adopted the demon lord's evil and vast power.

After many fireballs and lightning strikes, and one polymorph later, the demon lord conceded this was a sound strategy. Unfortunately this demon lord was a mere imitation, and it was eventually defeated.

Unfortunately, our heroes had more slime.

Wiser after the first battle, he attempted to mesmerize them, as they were very simple creatures. Unfortunately, as they were copies of him, they inherited his great resistance to magic. The ensuing battle destroyed much of the castle; frustrated, with a roar, he called down a great rock from the heavens, a secret technique of his, destroying his inferiors and the stones of the castle.

The demon lord took a breath, examined his destroyed castle, set up a few rocks for a wall, and then gave up.

Our heroes had commissioned the unemployed artists, through CGI, to create the same demon lord, with the same meteor-calling skill.

The demon lord was covered in a blinding light; he felt his flesh and bones set aflame; he tumbled many miles deep under the ground; his eyes were flooded with white light; now it was all dark. As he was created of pure evil, he slowly pulled the fibers of his flesh together, then his sinews, then his sensory organs, then his skin. Much exhausted, he groped out of the deep crater, unable to see light much of the journey; when he emerged, he saw our hero speaking to the doe; the doe approached the demon lord, and proposed to sell the castle, or, the ruins of his castle, for most of his fortune.

The demon lord set her aside, searched the cold night air, then slowly approached our hero. He proposed to our hero to end this eternity-long conflict with a duel, our hero's blood adequate enough to resolve this firmly. To him, this was a great humiliation, for he admitted in his heart that no adventurer had driven him so far, not even the warrior's party. As for our hero, he was horrified, and encouraged by the other heroes, who had far too high an estimation of his skills, and did not want to work anymore.

Our hero asked if he could use the restroom. The demon lord was too tired to deny him.

Much of the bathroom had been destroyed; only a mirror over a sink was left. Our hero stared deeply into the mirror, as this was the only thing able to save him. He saw hand sanitizer by the sink; he washed his hands very slowly.

Unbeknownst to him, the demon lord snuck behind him as

a fog. He had no intention of a fair fight, or rather, he felt to
survive was good and fair. He pinned our hero by his
shoulders, and gave him a menacing stare; our hero's body
was turned to stone. Yet the demon lord did not understand,
by way of the mirror, he turned himself too into stone; he had
many other things on his mind, caveats did not seem to fit in.

87

The stone of our hero's body began to crack; he emerged out of the shell; he breathed deeply, in a panic, in confusion; he then saw the world around him, the night air, the earth, and wondered how long he had been petrified. He came across the demon lord, also petrified, as his famous resistance to magic had been depleted after many arduous battles. Feeling something like pity, he broke the demon lord out; the demon lord did not desire to continue the fight, out of something like shame. They both surveyed the wide sky for a time.

They then perceived the world was very quiet, with only the wind whistling softly. The demon lord used his vast senses; he extended his hearing, and heard no birds; he placed his ear on the ground, and heard no worms; he yelled, and his sound returned back to him finding no one; he transformed his eyes into telescopes, and saw not a thing. He grew wings, picked up our hero, then placed our hero down, for he vomited from vertigo; he searched the lands, and found no souls, only empty wildernesses, empty wastes, empty kingdoms, empty villages, empty towns, ships sailing desolate, bedrooms emptied.

Our hero relayed to him what the goddess said, that the creator of the world, the god of gods, would destroy the worlds if the demon lords were not destroyed, which raised the demon lord's eyebrow. Our hero likened the state of the world to a developer deleting all of the player accounts in an MMORPG, yet leaving the world behind. The demon lord did not understand this analogy and thought our hero was stupid.

The demon lord, as was his nature, sought to rebuild his castle and his evil empire, and called our hero his slave. But our hero was incapable of everything, of architecting, of bricklaying, of even fetching water and food for himself. The demon lord was forced to do it all on his own, and sat in his empty throne room in his empty castle once more, with our hero giving him profuse praise.

Yet the demon lord felt empty. In fact, he felt disturbed; he did not understand why his creator would want him destroyed; he did not even consider, in his long existence, that he had a creator; he thought he *was*, and there was no more to it. He only wished to be evil; yet his creator let the world, in which he was evil, live on the contingency that he died; if there were no longer a world, he could no longer be evil; could it be that it was his fate to die? This was too much for him. He reasoned our hero was wrong, and sought to return back in time to the past.

This was easier said than done.

Our hero reasoned that this was the plot of one anime, where the developers shut down the servers for a time, then booted them back up for mysterious reasons after a software update, with the players returning. Perhaps, our hero reasoned, they should petrify themselves again, and hope that the world would be reset. This theory did not look good for the "developers", meaning, the creator of the world, seeing that he could not create new beings and regurgitated the old ones, but the demon lord had been arriving to the idea that the creator of the universe was not right in the head. He certainly could not be wise if he created our hero.

Before they would be petrified, our hero remarked on a beautiful flower, which neither had seen before or during the battle. This would be perfect for the goddess, this flower found at the end of time.

With the last of his magical energies, he petrified himself and our hero once more, and did not realize this time, unconsciously, he had no desire to wake up, for if he did, our hero would be correct.

Our hero was correct.

They both woke up on the exact same spot, in the exact same setting, in the exact same time no less, right after their great battle. The demon lord cursed our hero, and he cursed his creator, as much as he did not want to acknowledge this idea of one.

Our hero experienced a very different dilemma. He noticed his head was flaming.

88

Our heroes approached the demon lord, weapons in hand, and called him a coward, a chicken for tricking our hero, and sought to defeat him with their own strength, regardless of victory or defeat. To their surprise, the demon lord looked at them sadly and walked away, not to the ruins of his castle, not to the casino, but to the great expanse. The demon lord was defeated.

Our heroes celebrated; the city celebrated; the land celebrated; many older folks could not believe their eyes and ears; many younger folks felt finally there was hope for their children, who would never know of such evil; they cheered and feasted, and congratulated our heroes; many young, voluptuous, bosomy women wanted to make love to our hero, which propositions he accepted; out of courtesy, the citizens said his light novel was excellent; the land did not sleep for many days, there was so much joy; finally night swept into their eyes, our hero's loins were tired and dried, the mouths of many women were tired, and they slept.

When morning came, there was work to do. Our hero was tasked with proposing a business deal with a distant village.

Our hero traveled, in his mind relishing the day he would kill the businesswoman and take over the casino. He was disappointed he could not fly, and hired a horse carriage. The ride was bumpy, the driver was rude, and our hero had forgot to pack a lunch, for he had never eaten centuries before. Thus he realized that mortality was all thirst and stomach-grumblings and feeling too much heat or too much cold.

A sentry saw them; he sped away to the village; our hero did not mind, he believed the sentry was merely alerting the village of his arrival; he perceived the sentry was a goblin, and thought very little of it.

Arrows pierced the caravan; a sword beheaded the horse; spears were pointed at his person; he and the driver were captured. A goblin chief stripped our hero naked; he regaled the villagers with speeches concerning our hero's involvement in their genocide; they agreed to him being cooked alive so they may eat him; our hero was more distressed for he had never seen himself naked before, and how ugly his paunch and how small his male member were.

The villagers placed our hero over a pot that was not boiling yet, filled with delicious root vegetables, as potatoes and carrots, and leafy vegetables as cabbages. Our hero could see the horse's head floating in the pot. The goblins looked at him hungrily, and demanded the fire grow more quickly. In his prior existence, our hero would have had no fear, flames only tickled him; now fear actually struck him, as well as a contemplation on life after. He felt he was up for anything, even begging; he argued that he had eaten something foul, he would pollute the soup with bad odors; the goblins were persuaded, and inserted a large carrot in his rear, so that he would not pass gas in their meal.

Bubbles began dotting the water's surface. The goblins were resolute in removing his platform. He imagined to himself how much being boiled alive would hurt, with no hope of surviving, or, if surviving, being horribly impaired for the rest of his long life.

He closed his eyes; he felt a rush of cool wind around him;

he opened them; the bogwent rescued him, placing him on his back; the goblins cursed the bogwent, and cooked the driver instead.

The businesswoman was upset by the loss of the deal, yet was sympathetic and understanding. She recognized, too, that our hero was deeply disturbed by this adventure, and let him be.

89

When the demon lord petrified our hero and himself, he also swapped souls with our hero. Thus, he would reap the benefits of being our hero, whom fortune as of late greatly favored over the demon lord, and, without understanding it, hoped he could escape the fate his creator had in store for him.

Yet, after his most recent adventure, he found himself at an even greater loss. He confronted his mortality, it had never been so near before. When he walked past the city's mirrors, he found he was ugly; when he touched his belly, he knew he was fat; when he saw the looks of women, he knew his penis was small; and he found his ability to control women, control men, control fate was limited, that yesterday all these people loved him, and would do anything for him, but today they cared not a jot for him.

He was born with the world, when the earth was molten rock; he walked across pools of lava and rivers of magma, and, with his siblings, was lord of it all; when the rock cooled, and creatures formed, he ruled over them with an iron fist, being so much superior to them, then with a lax one, and only held them tightly when they needed to be reminded of who their master was; he perfected magic, it was so easy he yawned through it all, he found no need to write anything down; he created beings of his own, for he was greater than gods; he crushed those who thought they could be equal to him.

His favorite pastime was defeating adventurers. He

witnessed the males, strong in their youth, their chests puffed out, their muscles bulging, their faith great in their sword and their skill, and enjoyed handling them as a cat would handle a mouse, tortured them, then killed them. He witnessed the females, and forced himself on them, enjoyed seeing their belief in themselves, their control over their lives, drain from their eyes, enjoyed too the look in their lovers' eyes when they understood their powerlessness, seeing their wishes for a happy life destroyed. He enjoyed slaying children too, he enjoyed crushing kingdoms, empires, civilizations, for he hated the thing called hope, he hated that thing beings held onto, for he never perceived it himself, and thus it was not real.

He felt he himself was real, and everyone else was but a shadow. He enjoyed reminding the shadows of his reality.

Now, he stumbles on every rock; now, he panics when he hears the chirping of birds, in fear their droppings will fall on him; now, he fears being far from home, in case of hunger, thirst, or a need to relieve himself. Now his worries are real, where once, because of his awesome powers, he was able to blow them away, like the flame of a candle. He felt no sympathy for the humans, but now he realized he himself was not reality; horror is reality.

Why was he created? How must he live? Who created him? Why was he created the way he was? Why was he given so many great powers, only to be rendered powerless at the end? Why was he made evil, when it was better to make him good, make him in a way that didn't deserve to be destroyed? What is death? *Why* is death? Why?

Why could he not be empowered again; why could he not

be raised over humans again; why couldn't he be conqueror again? Then, the fear: if he was, he would reject it. His fate, to die, was inevitable. Or was his fate to die? Then what was his fate?

He said in his heart: I reject fate! I reject my creation! But it meant nothing in his soul, in fact, the idea felt absurd.

He touched the ruins of his castle. He felt every stone, considered the rooms they belonged to. He walked through his long life, a life of defeating, destroying, winning. It inspired neither happiness nor fondness in him.

He found his old cape, made of strengthened threads. He found a standing rock, standing just for him. He tied his cape to the rock, tied his neck to the other end, and hanged himself. He gasped; he was throwing a fireball at the first humans now; he choked, he was mesmerizing a town as his slaves; his face became blue; he laughed as he stabbed the soles of the adventurer's feet; he did not know what would come after, and he did not care; he breathed no more, then he passed on.

Our hero's soul then returned to his body; he panicked, and found the noose tight around his neck; he pulled on the cape with his hands, for he wanted to live; fortunately the rock collapsed, freeing him; unfortunately it fell on him, bludgeoning his head. The doe, who was concerned, ran to him, and tried to resuscitate him. He farted, she was glad.

90

The businesswoman felt now was the time to expand the business into distant lands. She reasoned there was a great opportunity in her homeland. She felt our hero would be the ideal ambassador.

Our hero agreed, as he had done so often in the past, and prepared to leave. He ensured the doe and the baby dragon were well-provided for, the mother dragon would have the lotion she needed for her non-CGI decaying skin, and the grandmother was taken care of unto her death.

As the businesswoman watched our hero prepare, she wanted to interrupt him, but she did not have the heart to stop him from happily stumbling through his preparations.

Need had always been her constant companion. She was the last child of five; two had died soon after birth, and one had died of illness later. Her father was absent; her mother, in her long grief, took to imbibing. She did not blame her mother for her negligence, because the lands had suffered a long famine before she was born. What little was grown or created was taken by the army and roving marauders.

She taught herself to steal. She dreamed of the day she would become the heroine she read about, the kind of person who stole from the rich and gave to the poor. For her wit and dexterity she was admitted into the Thief's Guild, and, because of the scruples of her teachers and fellow classmates, had not been whole since.

She would make some money, only for it to be taken from

her; she would be caught red-handed and required to pay ten times the stolen thing's amount at the cost of her head; she contemplated selling her body, not on the worth of its attractiveness, but on the depths of another's depravity; whatever friends she had met, were soon found to be fleeing with her gold. She was then asked to pay for her father's ransom, this very same figure whom she had never met, who could never be called a guardian, whom she knew nothing about, and she did so, out of the weakness in her heart, and in contemplating her weakness migrated to the lush forests in search of the meaning to her life.

She searched, in strangers' faces, the love that had been denied her, even when she made away with their gold. For she felt, even in her greatest moments of need, that money mattered so very little, though she hardly understood this.

Then she met our hero.

As she took his gold, she looked toward him. As she involved him in schemes, she looked toward him. As she sent him to certain doom, she looked at him. As she silently took over his business, she looked at him. She looked at him, realizing she sought in him love.

Even after knowing of his child, even when he married the doe, even when he cavorted with the dryad, she still looked at him, for she hadn't given up the hope that he would look back and return to her the love she had been missing. She little understood her feelings, yet she never attempted to understand, because she felt she could not go on without any love, whatever the quantity, whatever the intensity.

Now he was leaving, and she hadn't the heart to ask him to stay and return what was hers. She did as she had always done; she was looking at him. He was going away; soon he would be gone. She did not know how she would feel when this became fact.

She understood courage meant doing what the heart knew what had to be done. But she felt in her deepest of hearts that, if she declined to look at him now, she would be gone the second she looked away, and, one day, the well of memories would dry up and she would lose forever her image of love. She could only look. She understood this would be another wound in her heart, and though the wound may close, it will never truly heal.

Our hero set out. He waved goodbye to the businesswoman, the soldier, and the mage. He waved goodbye to the dragon princess. He waved goodbye to his fellow adventurers. He kissed the doe and the baby dragon goodbye. Then he departed into the sun with his caravan.

The mother dragon and the doe, despite being competing mothers, got along well. In fact, they made a little community with the sisters and their vampiric brides. Men scoffed and said women couldn't live without men, from a statistical standpoint, but they were happy nevertheless.

The businesswoman's affliction of being a dragon, oddly, did not go away with the demon lord's defeat. The affliction did not seem like an affliction at all, however, when it came time to secure deals with handshakes.

The soldier and his husband were quite pleased with one another on their isle on the sea; and when they were not, the soldier fought something until they were.

The mage enjoyed being a mother, yet found the task tiring; she was glad to have so many unemployed artists to gab with, who did make a small living from drawing animal pornography.

The water elemental continued serving as spa water, as she enjoyed male butts.

The dryad continued living for crossword puzzles, though she did not solve the very hard ones.

The new man survived and published a spoken-word album; this garnered him some admirers, whom he took some pleasure in sermonizing.

The giantess and the giant still fought a lot, but not as much as they had. Their daughter grew up to be whomever she wanted to be, except a helicopter pilot, which sufficed as one does not need a helicopter when living in the clouds.

The grandmother bought a new dog. They were visited once a year by the granddaughter.

The city government continued legislation for the city, proposing some good ideas, enacting many bad ones, on behalf of the rich and powerful. The citizens, nevertheless, lived their lives the best they could.

The fans of the demon lord missed him, yet they were content with his idol.

The tailor and the mummies struck a good relationship as artist and models.

The dwarves joined the sisters in their community, though they insisted they were just longtime friends.

The niece continued baking, not for the love of it, but for money.

Though the nightmare was known for being a mean person,

his experiences as a nightmare enabled him to be a great director, whose vulgarity was often forgiven.

The bogwent became the stuff of legends, for he minded his own business.

And so our hero moved on, with the flower he meant to give to the goddess, hoping that in the next life, he could begin the life of an adventurer as he has always desired.

And the world was not good, but it was, for this moment, glad.